ASSIGNMENT: AVALON

ASSIGNMENT: AVALON

SHADOWPAW PRESS *Attic*

Eddie Willett

ASSIGNMENT: AVALON

Published by
Shadowpaw Press
Regina, Saskatchewan, Canada
www.shadowpawpress.com

Ebook ISBN: 978-1-989398-27-2
Print ISBN: 978-1-989398-56-2

Cover design by Edward Willett
Created with Vellum

This book is dedicated to the Weyburn Review, where I was working when it was written.

I wrote this novel when I was in my twenties and working as a newspaper reporter/photographer for the *Weyburn Review* in Weyburn, Saskatchewan. Over the years, I've gone through it a couple of times, but it's never before been published.

Or, to put it another way, this is a novel by a younger, time-travelling version of myself who stole a time machine in the shape of a DeLorean around 1984 and came "back to the future" to take advantage of the publishing opportunities that didn't exist in his own time.

I hope you enjoy it!

Edward "Eddie" Willett
Regina, Saskatchewan
February, 2021

1 / BAILOUT

LIGHTS SWIRLED and sparkled around her head: cold blue for Preceptorate ships, bright green for rebels, yellow for outgoing missiles, and ominous red for incoming ones. Curved lines, marking trajectories, traced graceful webbing through empty space in a constant slow dance; flickering numbers and the computer's whispering voice in her ear described distances and speeds. And every so often, a light would flare and vanish, a trajectory tracer would fade away, and another ship and crew would be consigned to oblivion.

Melodan Castille picked her way through the deadly chaos with practised skill, fingers curling and twisting in the control gloves. A scattering of drones and ever-changing electronic jamming kept the missiles away as she deftly dodged debris, and her own missiles and beams cleared a path before her, straight to the brilliant red sphere that marked the Primary Target: *Charlemagne*, the flagship of Preceptor Johannes III himself.

Melodan boosted until the white line of her own trajectory marker neatly bisected the circle, ignoring the computer's sharp warning of imminent fuel exhaustion. She had enough for the attack—that was all that mattered.

She didn't see the trio of Preceptorate Swordcraft until she was within five hundred kilometres of the *Charlemagne*. They burst from behind the flagship and fanned toward her, filling her display with beams and missiles. She hesitated for only an instant—but her index finger was still curling to abort the attack when a red line touched the white blip of her ship. The screen flashed, then blanked.

Melodan swore and jerked off the virtual-space helmet. "Verbal input not understood," the computer's calm male voice murmured.

"You're not equipped for it anyway," she growled. "Display current status!" She stripped off the control gloves and reached for the glass of icefizz and the ham-and-cheese sandwich she had set on the communications console before starting the simulation.

Sipping the sweet liquid morosely, she leaned back in the form-fitting pilot's chair and scanned graphs and numbers on the flatscreens surrounding her on three sides. Nothing had changed since dimspace entry two and a half days before; every readout remained depressingly stable. After sixty hours of boredom, a small emergency would have been welcome—but she was too good a pilot.

"Then what am I doing *here*?" she asked herself. She tore a bite from the sandwich, and a mustardy bit of ham fell between her legs onto the seat's worn black vinyl. Swearing, she retrieved it. Scoutships, designed for long voyages, had to have artificial gravity so the pilot could function normally on the planet once he or she landed. Spaceplanes—what she *should* be flying—didn't. She preferred it that way.

She tilted her head back to drop the errant piece of meat into her mouth.

The movement brought her face to face with her reflection in the cockpit canopy, a shadow-Melodan surrounded by glittering console lights, hanging in the absolute blackness of dimspace. Grey eyes met grey eyes. "So you're stuck out here, too," Melodan said to shadow-Melodan. "I hope you're enjoying it more than I am." She smiled crookedly. "Tell you what—you fly on to Avalon, and I'll go back to the fleet. Deal?"

Shadow-Melodan did not look impressed.

Neither am I, Melodan thought. She jerked upright. A robot could perform this mission—on half power! "Replay simulation," she ordered the computer, then watched it unfold on the screen with bitter satisfaction. She'd come within seconds of single-handedly destroying—or at least damaging—the Preceptor's flagship. She'd never seen anyone do better in the "Preceptor's Last Stand" simulation. At the Academy on Alpha Centauri IV, she'd proven her skill over and over, graduating head of her class. If anyone had earned a combat assignment, she had. But when her orders came down? "Temporary scouting assignment." Scouting—when everyone knew the final attack on Earth was imminent.

The day before she left, all her classmates had received orders to report to the fleet. She had hoped, even then, that her own orders might be changed. Surely every pilot would be needed for the attack on Earth. But she had received no reprieve and had taken off on schedule from a rain-swept spaceport. No one had even seen her off. *They could be fighting right now*, she thought. *And here I sit—*

She gulped the rest of her icefizz, almost choking on it,

spun her chair, and slid through the cockpit's rear hatch into the cabin. The only touch of colour in the barren grey room was the thick blanket on the bed, the exact colour of bread mould. The bed took up one wall; a tiny desk and chair and a one-hot-plate galley filled the other. A toilet and shower were tucked behind a screen at the far end.

The depressing decor suited Melodan's mood. So did the air, scented with the unmistakable old-sock smell of a run-down recycler. Melodan flopped onto the bed and stared at the glowing ceiling for a moment, then reached onto the narrow shelf above her head and took down the only personal effect she had brought.

Her fingers ran in familiar, comforting fashion over the smooth surfaces of the glittering object, a scale replica of the powerful atmospheric/space fighters which had borne the brunt of battle on planet after planet during the century-long Revolution. Nothing ever happened in deep space; distances were too vast, ships too small. Battles were waged on and around planets, whose resources were vital to both sides.

Enter the spaceplanes. Carried between the stars by huge motherships, they swarmed in the skies over embattled planets, killing and dying in air and low orbit, softening defences so troopships could land infantry, attacking key industrial sites—and protecting the big ships from others like themselves.

Melodan's father had given her the model on her sixteenth birthday when he was home on Newhope on one of his infrequent leaves. They had ridden out from the family ranch on a frosty morning to the top of Hunchback Ridge to breathe the cinnamon-scent of the thunderpines and watch the sun rise over the mountains, chasing the triple moons from the sky.

Her father had reached into his saddlebag and drawn out something that shone in the golden light like a jewel. "Happy birthday," he said, handing it to her.

Melodan took it with awe. "It's beautiful," she whispered. She took off her glove and held it, icy cold, in her palm, her breath fogging its silver flank. "Where did you get it?"

"A pilot in my flight made them." He looked away. "He's dead now."

Melodan hardly heard him. "It's just like yours, isn't it?"

He nodded, his lean face glowing in the dawn light. "I'm glad you like it. I wasn't sure you would."

"Oh, Daddy, I love it!" Melodan carefully put it in her pocket.

"I know it's not very practical—maybe you can wear it on a chain or something."

"It will be my good-luck charm when I go to the Academy!" Melodan said impulsively.

Her father stiffened. "What?"

"I've decided, Daddy. I'm going to be a pilot—like you!" Melodan grinned at him, expecting him to be as excited as she was.

He sat very still for a moment, then said, "You're young. You'll change your mind."

She lost her smile. "But—"

"We'd better get back," he said harshly and turned his horse away. Hurt, she had trailed him home, and early the next morning had awakened to the sound of his shuttle roaring into the sky.

Melodan's fist closed over the model. She had not expected her mother to understand—but her father? Commander Garth Castille, a Revolutionary legend? All she had wanted was to be like him, to make him proud—but in the four years since, she had hardly seen him. He never visited her at the Academy, didn't even send her a hologram when she graduated—only a note with all the warmth of the form letter every graduate received from the Council.

Maybe if I were his son, she thought...*but he doesn't have a son. He only has me. And I'll never be good enough for him.*

And she certainly wouldn't prove otherwise with this mission. Sent to scout Avalon—a planet no one had been to in more than a century—just because some freighter intercepted an indecipherable signal. While meanwhile, the last great battle of the Revolution was shaping up. The last chance for combat. The last chance to show what she could do, to prove herself worthy of the Castille name.

"What did you do in the Revolution, Mommy?" she could hear her future children asking.

"I joined just in time for Battle of Earth," she'd tell them.

"And then what?" they'd ask.

"Then I scouted an empty planet while the rest of the pilots in my class wiped up the Preceptorate and came back with promotions and bonuses and medals, that's what!" she shouted to the empty cabin.

She slammed the model back on the shelf. *I'll bet Father is behind this. The big war hero—he'd know what strings to pull to keep me out of action. Probably even thinks he's doing me a favour—keeping me safe. Safely out of the way is more like it. He's afraid I'll prove him wrong!*

And she knew she could. She was *good,* in both space

and air. But while space piloting was an intellectual exercise, based on cold equations, with pilots providing the numbers and computers crunching them, atmospheric piloting was *real* flying. The scream of air under her spaceplane's wings was wild, exultant music to which she made the nimble craft dance.

But now she danced to someone else's tune—and she was sure her father paid the piper.

She banged a blue square on the wall with her fist, and the lights dimmed. All she could do was complete this nothing mission as quickly as possible and get back to the fleet. With luck, the Preceptor would hold out long enough for her to get her crack at him.

Closing her eyes, she settled in to sleep away the last eight hours of dimspace.

A SCREAMING alarm brought her tumbling out of bed before she was fully awake. She banged her shoulder on the bulkhead as she scrambled for the cockpit and, emerging into sunlight, knew she was back in normal space. But that wasn't what all the noise was about.

"Silence alarm!" she commanded the computer. "Display current status!" Rubbing her bruised shoulder, she searched the instruments for clues as to what was happening. At once, she saw a telltale energy trace on a screen to her left.

She was being scanned.

Avalon is too far away, she thought. *It must be a ship.* She squeezed into the control seat and pulled the virtual-space helmet down onto her head, then slipped her hands into the control gloves. But as she waved her hand to activate communications, a harsh new alarm buzzed, and the tactical overlay suddenly flashed on in the VS field. "Incoming missiles," the computer said. "First impact five minutes." To her upper right, a web of thin red lines spread out from an ice-blue blip, each line intersecting the white trail of her own trajectory. Next to the blue blip, a line of lettering appeared: "Preceptorate Cruiser, Class 7."

Melodan's mind went crystal clear. She could not fight or outrun a cruiser, or its missiles. She might evade one or two, but not six—and the cruiser could bring six *hundred* to bear.

"Missile ETA four and a half minutes," the computer informed her.

An empty feeling grew in her stomach. The first rule for any ship entering enemy territory was to have an escape course through dimspace pre-plotted. An attacker could not follow a dimming ship or determine its final destination.

But Melodan had not plotted such a course. Preoccupied with what she saw as her misfortune, convinced she was on a meaningless mission to an abandoned world, she had ignored that cardinal rule.

And now it was too late. Four minutes was not enough time to plot a course, and to dim without one would be suicide.

"Missile ETA three minutes, thirty seconds."

Melodan tossed the control gloves from her hands and pulled off the helmet so fast her ears burned. "Program lifeslip: meteor emulation, Avalon impact," she yelled at the computer, then spun and slapped a red button on the bulkhead. The cabin floor split apart, releasing a puff of cold, stale air, and revealing a padded, coffin-like container. Melodan snatched the spaceplane model from the shelf above the bed, then scrambled down into the lifeslip.

"Missile ETA three minutes," the computer said from a speaker by her ear. "Lifeslip programmed."

"Bailout!"

A metal shield snapped shut over her, plunging her into darkness. The artificial gravity cut off; she felt a slight bump, then a surge of acceleration.

The button to activate the final step of the bailout glowed green by her right hand, but Melodan didn't touch it, instead listening to the computer, transmitting from the abandoned ship.

"Missile ETA one minute. Lifeslip clear, on a trajectory for Avalon. Lifeslip ETA two hundred forty-four hours, twenty-seven minutes."

The acceleration ceased. Emitting no energy, insignificant in the vastness of space, the lifeslip should look like nothing but a meteor on any Preceptorate scanner. It would fire its engines again only if a mid-course correction were necessary.

Melodan hoped it wouldn't be: the tiny craft had little fuel, and she had bailed out at the extreme limit of its range. If not enough fuel was left to brake her descent...

"Missile ETA thirty seconds," the computer said, and though it was only a rather stupid artificial intelligence, Melodan admired the calm way it counted down the seconds to its own destruction. "Fifteen seconds. Ten. Nine. Eight. Seven. Six. Five." Melodan held her breath. "Three. Two. One."

A burst of static, then silence. The lifeslip continued its long fall. If the cruiser had detected it and was even then closing, Melodan would never know.

The blackness pressed in on her, and she was suddenly glad the lifeslip was not designed for a conscious passenger. Her breathing rasped in her ears, a counterpoint to her pounding heart. *Like being buried alive,* she thought, and wished she hadn't; the coffin-like container in which she was to spend the next ten days could yet become her real coffin.

She pressed the green button.

Thick liquid with the cloying smell of dying lilacs oozed all around her, and a needle stabbed her right arm through her thin shipboard coverall. Numbness swept out from the injection like an irresistible tide, and as the liquid closed over her mouth and nose, Melodan was dimly astonished that she felt no panic, nor any desire to breathe.

A moment after that, she felt nothing at all.

Kyla XA294 stood very still in the middle of the immense, circular room. Whispers and distant noises made eerie by echoes swirled around her, playing hide and seek among the green marble pillars that separated the great white dome of the ceiling from the flat white expanse of the floor. Directly overhead hung a giant crystal chandelier, and she was struck by the unreasonable fear that it would fall and crush her if she dared to move.

"Wait here," she'd been told by the sour-faced middle-aged woman who had greeted her and led her to this spot, then had disappeared up the wide, black-carpeted staircase Kyla now faced, the only interruption in the equidistant spacing of the pillars along the walls. The room had no furniture, but several closed shiny black doors punctuated the walls behind the pillars. A hint of something like incense, but bitter, not sweet, hung in the chill air.

Kyla had never imagined a place so grand, so beautiful—and so utterly without human warmth. If a house reflected its owner, she hated to think what this room said about her new mistress, Lady Ava Moldar.

The distant noises continued to tease her ears, but still, no one appeared on the black stairs. Kyla shifted her stance a little, keeping a wary eye on the threatening chandelier. *Whatever Lady Moldar is like*, she thought, *this place has got to be better than the tekfarm. And at least I'll be closer to Tor...*

Her twin had always dreaded the day, inevitable though it was, when Skandar, the artificial intelligence that managed tek society, assigned them their lifetasks. Whenever they were alone, he had railed against Skandar, against the Strator, who set the policies Skandar carried, against the Noble Council that advised the Strator, against the lords and ladies that all teks served, against a system that offered them no choice of futures.

He'd talked of running away, of joining the semi-mythical "Free Forcers" who supposedly were conducting a guerilla war against Skandar and the Strator, or, if the Free Forcers really didn't exist, of starting such a war himself. But locked within the tekfarm's fence, constantly watched by Thoughtforcers and worked long and hard in the fields, talk was all it had ever been.

Three months ago, he'd been given his lifetask, before she received hers; unusual, but who knew why Skandar did anything? And it had been the worst possible news, considering how Tor felt: he'd been assigned to Skyforce, the aerial arm of the province's military. He would be serving the hated Skandar and the Strator directly; might even be asked to kill and die for them on the Battlefield, in the never-ending struggle against the other provinces, who would like nothing better than to divide up Skandar's riches among themselves.

He must have been miserable these last three months, she thought. She hoped she could cheer him up. She'd already sent a message to Skyforce Base, telling Tor she'd finally been assigned her lifetask, maidservant to Lady Moldar, and when she would arrive. He might already have sent a message to her here...she shifted her weight again. Maybe the Lady would even let her go visit Tor right away. Of course, she'd have lots to learn about her duties here for the first little while, but surely Lady Moldar could spare her for a few hours...

Surely Lady Moldar could have spared her a chair, too. She'd already had a long trip from the tekfarm, and only the last half-hour of it had been on good roads. Her muscles ached from jouncing over potholes for two hours before that. How long would she be kept waiting?

Not the proper mindset for a servant, she admonished herself. Didn't people talk about servants waiting on their masters "hand and foot?"

She just hadn't realized the phrase could be meant so literally.

She looked hopefully up the stairs...and at last, her patience was rewarded. The sour-looking servant returned. "Follow me," she said.

She led Kyla up the steps—up close, the black carpet was improbably thick and soft, almost like fur—to a landing where the steps split left and right while a broad corridor continued straight ahead. They followed the corridor, whose black carpet, white walls, and black doors were relieved only by thin green piping along the baseboard and around the doorjambs. Kyla found the decor hideous. Maybe she'd get used to it.

As if she had a choice.

The incense-liked smell grew stronger as they walked. Several doors and a couple of ugly abstract jade sculptures later, Kyla's guide stopped by a door that, unlike all the others they had passed, stood open. "In there," the servant said. Kyla stepped in, and the servant closed the door behind her without entering.

Kyla coughed, finding the bitter smell almost overpowering here. She stood in a small, dark room, facing a wall on which images moved.

In front of the huge vidscreen, a woman sat on a black leather chair, behind a curved console of pale wood that glittered with hundreds of tiny lights. "Lady Moldar...?" Kyla ventured.

"Quiet," the woman snapped. "I have a wager riding on this." To her right, something glowed inside a glass sphere atop a waist-high wooden tripod. Curls of bitter smoke rose lazily from holes in the top of the sphere, and from one of those holes snaked a silvery tube. Lady Moldar lifted it to her lips and sucked the smoke into her lungs, holding it there for a moment before releasing it through her nose, never taking her eyes from the vidscreen.

There, a ship floated in a little cove, in water so smooth Kyla could see the stars reflected in it, though beyond the ship, beyond the rocky shores of the cove, the white curls of breakers rolled across the sea.

Long-fronded tropical trees framed the image, and from somewhere in the forest came the long, mournful, descending cry of an animal, heartbreakingly lonely...and heartbreakingly lovely. For a moment, Kyla wished more than anything that she was on that ship, in that beautiful cove.

But then she heard another sound, a harsh, mechanical buzzing. Hatches suddenly banged open on the ship, and people swarmed onto its deck, shouting, pulling canvas off lumps she'd taken for fishing equipment but now saw were missile launchers and guns. For the first time, she realized this was a Seaforce ship, and the image must be coming from the Battlefield. Which meant the buzzing...

Searchlights stabbed up from the ship, bringing a dozen diving Skyforce planes into sharp relief against the black sky. An instant later the planes opened fire. Tracers slashed blood-red streaks through the darkness and raked the length of the ship. Kyla stared, horrified, as men tumbled like broken dolls across the splintering deck, spraying blood into the scuppers, splashing into the cove to float and bob like so much driftwood.

The ship's guns returned fire. Tracers chased the aircraft back into the sky, and missiles hissed after them like fiery, angry snakes. Plane after plane spun and tumbled from the sky or exploded in mid-air, blooming into orange fireballs like giant, evil flowers. None survived to make a second pass.

The gunfire ceased, and silence descended on the scene once more...but a thick pall of smoke hid the stars, and now the bloody water only reflected the fires burning on the ship's scarred deck.

The image vanished. Lady Moldar laughed. The sound scraped Kyla's nerves like a wire brush across sunburned skin. "I win again!"

Kyla's stomach churned. Lady Moldar had been

wagering on the outcome of that battle...wagering on death. Kyla stared at her new mistress. She looked ordinary enough —too much makeup, black hair too perfectly groomed, but that was just the ordinary unnaturalness of every lord or lady Kyla had ever seen. Nevertheless, Kyla felt like she was looking at a monster in human clothing. How could anyone bet on bloodshed?

And then she remembered that among those who had died had been twelve Skyforcers...and Tor was in Skyforce.

She *had* to see him, *soon*, had to tell him what she had seen in this room. Everything he'd always said about teks being nothing more than slaves...it was even worse than he'd thought. If he knew—if *all* the Forcers knew—that the lords and ladies were betting on their battles, that the Battlefield was only a game to them...she didn't know what they'd do. She didn't know what they *could* do. But surely, they would do *something*!

Lady Moldar touched her console, and the room lights came up, momentarily blinding Kyla. The Lady studied her critically. "You'll do," she said after a moment. "Young, strong, not too bad to look at...I won't be ashamed to show you in public, unlike that last tek Skandar tried to palm off on me." She stood up abruptly. "You've met Hildar?"

"Hildar?" Kyla said. "Milady," she added hurriedly.

"The one who brought you in. She's in charge of the household. She'll explain your duties to you and show you around the estate." Lady Moldar touched another control on the console. "She'll be back momentarily." She lifted the smoke-tube again.

Kyla took a deep breath, then wished she hadn't as the smoke-stained air threatened to choke her. She cleared her throat; swallowed. "Milady, may I ask a favour?" she said finally.

Lady Moldar raised an eyebrow. "I'm not in the habit of granting favours to servants I have just met."

"I know, milady, I'm sorry, I wouldn't ask, but...I have a twin brother in Skyforce. May I take a couple of hours tomorrow and go see him at Skybase, just to let him know where I am and that I'm all right? He left the tekfarm three months ago—Skandar gave him his lifetask early. We've never been apart this long before."

Lady Moldar's lips tightened, and for a moment, Kyla was certain she was going to say no, but then the Lady relaxed and shrugged. "Why not? But you won't get to see him very often, uh...Kyla, is it?"

"Yes, milady."

"You'll have many duties to keep you busy...and in a few days, I'll be moving the household to my mountain estate for the autumn to oversee the coralsap harvest. There's much to be done before that can happen, and then we'll be up there for at least two months. However, you may go tomorrow. I'll tell Hildar."

"Thank you, milady."

Lady Moldar was true to her word, and Kyla thought slightly better of her employer the next day as she crossed Skandar City in an automated wheeler, marvelling at the sights: towers reaching up to the clouds, or so it seemed, parks where fountains glittered among magnificent beds of flowers, shops whose windows revealed tantalizing glimpses of clothes more beautiful than she'd ever imagined...

But the streets were all-but-deserted, and as the wheeler continued to roll through the city, she found herself thinking about the tekfarm, the run-down dormitory room she and Tor had shared, the wooden shacks that were all the farmteks had to call their own...and the acidcore fence that penned them there.

All the teks in Skandar province could be living in this half-empty city, instead of in hovels behind fences, she thought bitterly. *Tor was right: we're just slaves, slaves to Strator Artega, his pet artificial intelligence, and the nobles. Nobles who watch teks die in battles the lords and ladies started and then bet on the results. Tor's always hated the Forcers and the nobles, and now he's in Skyforce. It must be killing him.*

She looked out the window again, this time not at the beautiful park she was passing but the mountains rising in the distance.

Maybe we could *run away,* she thought. *Just the two of us...we could hide up there forever, and all the Forcers Skandar has wouldn't be enough to find us...and why would they even care? Two teks, more or less...who would notice? Surely the Strator has enough to worry about without wasting Forcers on us.*

I'll ask Tor. Oh, there's Skybase...

TOR SAT in the Skybase mess hall, deserted at this hour of the afternoon except for a thin, gaunt-faced tek scrubbing the floor behind the serving counter in a desultory fashion. The sharp smell of ammonia pinched at Tor's nostrils.

From his table, Tor gazed out large glass windows over rows of parked aircraft, the vast landing field, the spaceport control tower, the security wall—and above all, the sky: blue, serene, dotted with clouds so purely white you could tell just by looking at them they'd never been sullied by contact with the ground.

That sky called to him. This was the first afternoon since he'd earned his wings that he hadn't been up flying with Parl and the others he had started his training with three months ago. Up there, he could forget...everything. Everything that had happened, everything that might happen. The tekfarm...the Battlefield...

But here, on the ground, it was all too real. And his sister...

His sister would make it all that much *more* real.

He heard the door open behind him, but he didn't turn around. He heard footsteps start toward him, walking at first, then running, but still, he didn't turn around until those footsteps slowed, then stopped, and his sister's voice said uncertainly, "Tor? Is that..."

Slowly, he stood and turned. "Hello, Kyla."

"Tor!" She flung herself on him, and he put his arms around her reflexively. His heart lurched inside his chest. He was glad to see her, of course he was glad, but...

It wasn't...the same. Not the same as before.

Before he could fly.

Kyla broke free and stepped back, wiping her eyes. "Tor...that uniform...I'm so sorry."

Tor looked down at the blue Skyforce uniform, blue as the sky outside the window, and fingered the red-glazed glass wings pinned over his heart. "It's not so bad. I've gotten used to it."

Kyla dropped her voice to a whisper and leaned in close.

"Tor, I've seen the most horrible things at Lady Moldar's. We have to get out of here—out of this city, hide in the mountains. Just you and me. You were right, right about everything."

Tor rubbed the back of his neck. "Let's sit down."

Kyla plopped down in the chair where Tor had been sitting. He would have preferred to sit there himself, where he could see the sky, but instead, he took another. Kyla was upset. He had to calm her down before she did something stupid, something that might jeopardize what he'd found here.

"Tell me what you saw," he said in a low voice.

She told him about watching a vidcast at Lady Moldar's estate, a Skyforce attack on a Seaforce ship—no notion of which province's ships and planes they were, of course, civilians never noticed things like that—and about Lady Moldar wagering on the outcome. "That's when I knew," she said, her voice becoming dangerously loud and excited. The tek scrubbing the floor looked up and frowned. "I knew you were right! Everything you ever said about—"

He made a sharp hushing motion with one hand, and she lowered her voice again just in time, though her gestures remained agitated.

"Everything you said about Skyforce, about the nobles, about Skandar. We really are just slaves, Tor. I saw the city—there's no one in it. Teks should be living in those fine towers, shopping in those stores, eating at those restaurants. We shouldn't be locked up on tekfarms and sent to die on the Battlefield just for the amusement of people like Lady Moldar!"

It was worse than he thought. If anyone else heard her

say these things, heard her attribute these ideas to him...he'd never fly again. They'd send him back to the tekfarm, or into the mines, or worse.

He took her angry hands, held them still in his, and tried to still her angry thoughts as well. "Kyla, I was wrong," he said soberly. "Being here, I've learned...I've learned things I never understood before. Teks have to fight on the Battlefield. We fight on behalf of everyone."

Kyla stared at him as though he'd suddenly sprouted a second head. "You really think that?"

He met her gaze steadily. "Of course, I do! Kyla, until I came here, I didn't realize the danger of failure on the Battlefield. The other provinces envy us. Skandar is the richest on Avalon. If we lose on the Battlefield, someone will attack us for real—and then a lot more people will die. Civilian people, not the lords and ladies, who can always get away. Teks."

Kyla's face had gone pale, and she jerked her hands free. "Those aren't your words! They're Skyforce's!"

"That doesn't mean they're not true."

"But, Tor—you've always hated Forcers. You—if I hadn't talked you out of it, you would have tried to run away that night they gave you this lifetask. You said you didn't care if they whipped you. You said—"

"I know what I said," Tor snapped. *She doesn't understand*, he thought bitterly. *How can she?* "But now I know better. I can't turn my back on Skyforce. I'd be a coward. And a traitor."

Kyla stared at him, white and wide-eyed. The janitor-tek dragged his mop-bucket out through the mess hall's swinging doors, taking the smell of ammonia with him. A trio of

Skyforce fighters roared overhead; Tor glanced at the window in time to see them traverse the patch of heartbreakingly blue sky in perfect formation. When he looked back at Kyla, the colour had come back into her face with a vengeance, and her eyes had narrowed. "You *like* it here," she accused him. "You don't *want* to leave.'

"I can *fly*, Kyla. You can't imagine what it's like—I couldn't, before. Freedom, control—down here I'm just a tek —up there I'm a lord!"

"Until they send you to the Battlefield! Until they start wagering on your death! Don't you see, Tor?" Her voice turned pleading. "They're brainwashing you. Flying...it's like a drug, to make you stay. Fight it, Tor! Come away with me, now. We can escape! The wheeler will take us through the gate. Then we can run—into the fields, up into the mountains. No one could find us—"

She reached out for him, but he pushed her hands away, irritated to the verge of anger. She not only didn't understand, she never *could* understand. Never. He stood up, the chair scraping across the polished floor. "No, Kyla. I think you should go now."

Kyla jumped up, her own chair clattering backwards, her fists clenched, glaring at him. Tor hated to see her so angry with him. Always before, on the tekfarm, he'd been there to comfort her, to take her in his arms and tell her everything would be all right, even when he couldn't do anything.

Not this time. They weren't the same people they had been. They weren't children any longer. He held himself stiffly, almost at attention. "It was good to see you."

"Was it?" she said tightly. "It wasn't good to see you, Tor. It wasn't good at all."

She turned sharply, kicked the chair out of her way—knocking two more over in the process—and stormed out. Tor almost called after her but then held his tongue. What could he say? She wanted him to run away, and he wouldn't.

Couldn't.

She disappeared through the swinging doors, and he glanced at the clock above the serving counter. 1429. He could still get in two hours of flying. With luck, he might even catch Parl on the ground, and they could fly together.

He returned the fallen chairs to their places with military precision, then headed for the flight line.

3 / "THAT'S NO METEORITE!"

THE LIFESLIP FELL STEADILY toward Avalon, inert and cold. Inside, the computer patiently counted the seconds to the braking manoeuvre. Its programming had been perfect; no mid-course correction had been required.

On board the Preceptorate Battle Cruiser *Bloodline*, a bored ensign once again checked the trajectory of In-System Object 224, as he had checked the trajectory of every one of the two hundred twenty-three tracked objects before it and the four hundred forty-nine objects after it three times already that shift. If one of those objects unexpectedly changed course, they'd have Swordcraft after it in minutes...but none of them ever did. Even if they did, the computer would surely notice it before he did. But regulations required a human being to doublecheck the computers, so here he sat, staring at a screen full of multicoloured lines until his eyes went numb.

He stiffened as the First Officer, making his rounds of the bridge stations, leaned over his shoulder. "Anything interesting, Ensign?"

"No, sir."

"What's that?" The First Officer pointed to the trajectory he'd just highlighted.

"Meteor, sir. We've been tracking it for ten days."

"Looks like it's headed for an Avalon impact."

"Yes, sir. I was just wondering if we should warn them, sir." Actually, he hadn't been wondering any such thing, but suggesting it might earn him a few points...

The First Officer laughed. "Let them worry about it. That fancy AI of theirs, what's-its-name, Skandar, is supposed to be able to deflect any meteors that pose a danger. And if it can't...well, the baron will want to know, since our whole mission depends on that computer." He straightened. "Don't warn Avalon, Ensign...but keep an eye on that object. I want to know what happens when it hits the atmosphere. Carry on."

"Yes, sir." The ensign coded the computer to signal him when the object was two hundred kilometres above the planet, then un-highlighted its trajectory and moved on to the next.

Inside the lifeslip, Melodan slept without dreaming.

EKLAND ARTEGA KEPT his face impassive, but his hands, out of sight of the haughty eyes of the dark-skinned young man in his desktop vidscreen, clenched the wooden arms of his worn leather chair. "Really, Strator," the young man was saying in a bored tone, "your problems with petty terrorists are of no concern to the Preceptorate. The Preceptor's fleet can hardly be threatened by plastic rifles."

"The threat is not to the Preceptor's fleet, Baron Markus, but to my control of this province," Artega replied, his voice even, his hands clenching ever-more-tightly. "This *should* concern you because I control Skandar. Should I be replaced, you would lose the data link you require to successfully refortify this system before the Preceptor's arrival."

The baron grimaced as though he smelled something distasteful. "Exactly what is it you want, Strator?"

"You already know." Artega leaned closer to the vidscreen. "Weapons, space-based reconnaissance, communications equipment."

Markus shook his head. "I'm afraid it's all out of the question. You must understand, Strator, I have only one ship, half a dozen Swordcraft, and scant weeks to do what normally takes half a fleet half a year. And need I remind you of the Rebel scoutship I destroyed just ten days ago? I must remain on station near the dimspace nexus in case some other Rebel pilot bumbles into this system in search of his lost comrade. My Swordcraft must inspect every component of the system defences, effecting repairs as necessary. I simply cannot take time to boost to Avalon to help you do something you should be perfectly capable of doing on your own." He pointed one slender finger at Artega. "And please, Strator—don't threaten me again. If you disrupt my data link, I *will* boost in—and blow you and your whole decadent city into orbit." He smiled. "After all, if I lose that link, I can't do what the Preceptor has ordered me to do, and in that case, I have nothing to lose. Do you understand?"

Artega nodded, barely.

The baron began examining his silver-painted fingernails one by one. "Good. I assure you, Artega, when the Preceptor arrives, his soldierserfs and Swordcraft will make short work of your so-called terrorists. You'll just have to do the best you can until then. Now, if you'll excuse me—" He reached forward, and the screen blanked.

Artega swore. It was his usual reaction to Baron Nevel Markus, commanding the Preceptorate Battle Cruiser *Bloodline*. It had been his reaction a month earlier, when Skandar, the artificial intelligence on which Artega's rule depended, had interrupted a report on fish production with the unprecedented announcement that a message from space had just been received, and Artega had met Baron Markus for the first time.

Markus had been succinct. He had informed the Strator that starships had stopped coming to Avalon a century ago because of a revolution within the Preceptorate, that the revolution now threatened Earth, and that the Preceptor had chosen Avalon as his new capital and refuge.

"Why?" Artega asked. "You've ignored us for decades. You left us here to rot!"

"Planetary defences, my dear fellow," said Markus. "System defences—the best outside of Earth. The duke who set up Avalon as a pleasure planet for nobles held a highly unorthodox view of exactly who should succeed the Preceptor of his day and knew a number of high-level military suppliers who agreed with him. Alas, a revolution quite different from the one he intended upset his plans, and the defences he built were never activated—but here they are. Killer satellites, sensors, missile platforms—brainy asteroids, beamers—everything one could want, really."

Artega frowned. "I've never heard—"

"Of course not. Such defences under the private control

of one noble were highly illegal. I imagine your AI is programmed to suppress any mention of them that might surface within your datanet. Had the duke in question been in residence on Avalon when the Revolution began, he would probably have seized control from the planetary administrator—Strator, to you—and activated the system, but he was visiting a lord admiral at the Preceptorate base on Evershine Prime and had the misfortune of being on the surface when a Rebel tacnuke dropped out of orbit.

"The rebels never bothered to attack Avalon—just a metal-poor resort planet, after all, as far as they or anyone else knew. They just blockaded you and jammed your communications. All the starships left on Avalon took off; none made it back to Preceptorate space. The Preceptorate assumed the planet had been taken. We only recently learned differently from a freighter captain who swung through your system to scoop up hydrogen. Some bright fellow did some research and discovered hidden records of these defences. And here I am." Markus had spread his ringed hands. "I'm here to turn them on."

That was the beginning, Artega thought bitterly. *From ruler of Skandar province to valet of an effeminate Preceptorate Forcer.*

He looked around his office, at the deep-red carpet, the dark-panelled walls, the bar with its sparkling crystal carafe of Odelphian wine, the desk/computer that linked him with Skandar. He breathed deep the familiar smell of wood and leather. It smelled like power...and it smelled like home.

He had worked thirty-five years to get where he was. The youngest son of a minor noble, he had chosen early on to enter the service of Strator Thurgood Gelff rather than waste his time in the idle pursuits of his three older brothers. He had perceived quite clearly that power did not, as most supposed, lie with the Noble Council, an ossified group of elderly lords and ladies who were descendants of the seven lords who had backed Petra Ignobar in his forceful assumption of power in the early days of Avalon. Artega had seen then that the real power was in the hands of the man who controlled Skandar, the artificial intelligence—and that man was Strator Gelff.

But the Strator also had to be able to control the Council. Through years of diligence, Artega had undermined Gelff while maintaining an image of loyalty. He had been prepared to manufacture a crisis in order to finally convince the Council to remove Gelff, but in the end, it had not been necessary—the crisis had come on its own.

It was ironic that the very "terrorists" he now denounced to Markus were responsible for his assumption of power. The "Free Forcers," as they called themselves, were originally Groundforcers, soldiers of Skandar, but they had deserted under the leadership of their commander, a man named Rand. And Gelff had been unable to punish them— or even to find them.

That humiliation had been enough to get him removed, though, of course, the official story was that he had resigned for "personal reasons." The Council turned naturally to Artega, his second-in-command, whom they knew for his unswerving loyalty and devotion. In the fifteen years since, he had ruled firmly, consolidating his power, and it pleased him that while he was the most powerful and wealthiest man on the planet, his brothers were the most impoverished nobles, having wasted their father's meagre inheritance gambling. He provided them with small allowances and laughed to think how it must gall them.

The only thorn in his side was the Free Forcers. For a long time, he had heard nothing of the deserters and had assumed they had starved in the mountains. But then reports had started coming in of teks deserting farms near the mountains, of sabotage on the Battlefield, of stolen weapons and equipment, and finally of the greatest outrage of all—raids on noble estates.

And while Artega was struggling with that problem, coldly aware it could bring him down as it had his predecessor, Markus had come.

The arrival of the *Bloodline* had changed everything—and nothing. Only Artega knew the ship orbited their star. "Someone might take the notion to warn the rebels," said the baron. "They could do it from your spaceport."

As a result, Artega had to carry out his duties as always. He found it blackly humorous to be dealing with corn production and the transportation of potash when Avalon's entire society was about to be swallowed by the Preceptorate. And the one task which still mattered, the suppression of the Free Forcers, Markus refused to assist him with.

He sighed and looked at the list of things to do that had replaced the baron's face on his desk screen. "Skandar, Battlefield report," he said, thinking as he did so that here was the most useless example of business-as-usual. The principle of the Battlefield, that the half-dozen provinces of Avalon could settle their differences on neutral ground instead of destroying each other, seemed ludicrous with interstellar war about to erupt around them.

His screens lit with a cratered and smoking landscape,

somewhere beyond the mountains. Bodies littered the shattered ground amid the blackened hulks of wheelers. "Casualty comparison," he said.

Bright green numbers replaced the image of destruction on one screen. Artega leaned forward. "Nordel lost fifty more teks than Orstend," he said. He was Strator of all Avalon, of course, but he kept a close eye on the Battlefield fortunes of his home province of Nordel. "General Everlon's worst-case prediction was for equal losses."

"The error is statistically insignificant," replied Skandar's deep, disembodied voice. "Although Nordel's tek casualties were high, note that Orstend lost eight more gunwheelers and six aircraft. I have rated this a minor victory for Nordel."

"Hmmph." Artega touched another control and the screens cleared. "In-province security report."

"No new disturbances. News of the recent raids on mountain estates has so far been effectively withheld from the tek population."

The Strator grunted. "That won't last. Too many nobles know about them—the Council is already becoming impatient. And what masters know, servants somehow always find out." He scratched the bridge of his nose irritably. *Blast Markus for refusing to help!* "Increase Skyforce reconnaissance and move some Groundforcer scouts up there. Next time there's a raid, I want trackers on the scene within hours. We have to find where these 'Free Forcers' are based."

"Yes, Strator."

"Next subject. Has the production shortfall in the northwest oil field been rectified?"

"Yes, Strator. There were insufficient workers; I trans-

ferred a hundred prisoners from the labour camp at—"
Abruptly, the computer's voice ceased.

Artega stared at the walls. "Skandar?" Nothing. "Skandar, answer!"

After a moment of tense silence, the computer replied, "Strator, orbital sensors detect a large meteor approaching from the west. Initial predictions indicate impact in the immediate vicinity."

"In the city?"

"Possible. Readying meteorite deflectors." Artega leaned forward, but almost immediately, Skandar said, "Abort. Deflection unnecessary. Object will impact in the ocean." Skandar paused again. "Revision. Object is not a meteor. Predicted impact area now the mountains."

Artega stiffened. "Repeat!"

"Object is not a meteor. Predicted—"

"Explain!"

"Object altered course to avoid ocean impact. This indicates either computer or human guidance." Another pause. "Object is over Skandar province. Crossing city. Braking..."

Artega held his breath.

"Impact."

"Where?"

"Peak 897W1, due east, eighty kilometres." Pause. "Analysis of descent indicated small spacecraft on landing approach. However, landing occurred at a rate of speed outside normal spacecraft operating parameters."

"You mean it crashed?"

"Available data are consistent with that interpretation."

Artega's hands tightened on the arms of his chair. Ten days ago, Baron Markus had destroyed a Rebel scoutship.

Now a spacecraft had crashed in the mountains. There had to be a connection.

The Strator reached out a hand to call the *Bloodline*, then stopped. *Right now, the baron holds all the cards*, he thought. *But if this is another Rebel ship, and the pilot survived...I could have a trump. Or at least a bargaining chip.*

He pulled his hand back. "I want Skyforce at the crash site at first light. And Groundforce as soon as possible. I want the ship—and I want the pilot. Alive."

"Yes, Strator."

Artega leaned back, folding his hands across his grey-clad stomach. When the starships had stopped coming, the Strator of the day had been unable to adapt. Chaos had resulted; only when Ignobar and his accomplices killed the Strator and took control had order been restored, the old society altered to meet the new demands.

Now the world was changing again. But unlike the Strator who had failed and died, Artega intended to change with it—and keep control.

***

On board the *Bloodline*, the ensign looked up from his scanner at the First Officer. "Skandar did it, sir," he said. "The meteor altered course at the last minute. Skandar's deflectors must be working."

"Excellent," said the First Officer. "I'll tell the baron. Good work, Ensign."

Pleased, the ensign turned back to his station. Maybe he'd scored a few points after all...

He cleared the meteor's trajectory from his board and returned to the grind of double-checking all the others.

Colonel Arthur Rand, Commander of the Free Forces of Avalon, lay belly-down in sopping wet leaves, ignoring both the multi-legged crawler creeping up the bridge of his nose and the drop of sweat running down it, though a portion of his brain commented, as it always did just before a raid, that he was getting too old for this...

He could see nothing in the darkening twilight but thick underbrush in all directions, even though he knew three men and two women lay concealed within a radius of four metres. He would have nodded approvingly if he'd allow himself to move more than his eyes.

Where was Vik? He'd promised himself long ago he wouldn't treat his son any differently than any other Free Forcer recruit, but his heart didn't believe it. The boy had been gone a long time. What if he'd been caught?

They'd have heard something. Vik wouldn't have given up without a fight, without shouting a warning to the others. He was only being thorough, scouting the scene as Rand had taught him. He'd grown up out here in the woods. Rand was more likely to be caught than he was...

And then, suddenly, there he was, his green-daubed face materializing in the underbrush barely a metre away. His eyes, expressionless, met his father's. He nodded once, turned, and squirrelled away again.

Rand raised his head, wincing slightly—damn, he *knew*

better than to let himself stiffen like that!—and lifted a clenched fist. Then he crawled after his son.

The woods ended ten metres away in a fence—ordinary plastic mesh, not that acidcore abomination they used on the tekfarms. Vik waited by the neat man-sized opening he had cut in it. Beyond the mesh and twenty metres of bare dirt rose the blank wall of an equipment shed; beyond that, and a vast expanse of smooth, blue-green lawn, the white brick of a sprawling house seemed to glow in the fading light. Its pillars and high arched windows spoke of wealth and power. Two rooms were lit. Rand could see no movement in them, but from somewhere, there drifted an occasional snatch of music, mingled with laughter.

The darkened rooms actually concerned him more; he watched their windows warily. A Groundforce platoon could be hidden inside, and they'd never be able to tell.

But Vik, scouting ahead earlier in the day, had seen teks unloading explosives into that shed, the kind used for clearing tree stumps, and Rand couldn't afford to pass up any chance to replenish their supplies.

He glanced at Tara on his right and Starax on his left and nodded to them both. They looked at each other, gripped their rifles, then together scrambled up and dashed across the open space toward the shed.

No reaction from within the house. They reached the shed. After they took quick glances around both ends, Starax kept watch while Tara slipped around to the white-painted wooden door. Five seconds—she really was very good at that sort of thing, Rand thought, a legacy of her misspent youth dodging Peaceforcers in Skandar City—and she had the door open.

Rand raised his hand, and four more Free Forcers scurried across the open ground to the shed. While Starax continued to watch the house, they disappeared inside and emerged carrying small grey boxes. Five minutes after they'd emerged from the forest, they faded back into it.

Safely away from the house and finally able to walk upright again, Rand congratulated the seven men and five women who made up his raiding party...and almost half of the fighting strength of the Free Forcers, though he preferred not to think about that. "Good work, son," he added privately to Vik as they spread out into double file again.

Vik shrugged off the praise silently and pushed forward to the second rank. Rand scratched at his heavy, grey-flecked black beard in frustration. He couldn't figure the boy out. He did a fine job as a Free Forcer, but Rand could hardly even get him to talk. From what he understood, he hardly talked to anyone else, either.

Not since his mother died.

Painful memories. Rand pushed them aside. Winter thoughts, he called them, those bleak doubts and second-guesses that crowded his mind through the long, cold nights like black birds. Winter was coming, but it hadn't arrived yet. Summer was the time for fighting, and in two days, they'd strike their most telling blow yet against Ekland Artega and his pet AI.

Full night descended quickly, but Rand had a nearby site in mind for their camp and a clear path to take them to it, along a stream flowing down a gully that deepened rapidly. Only Tara, on point, used a flashlight, hooded to keep light from escaping up to where a Skyforcer reconnaissance balloon might be silently hanging. An hour after sunset,

Rand made his way to the front of the column and stopped Tara. "Shine your light over there," he said, pointing to the right. She did so, the beam revealing stone, dirt, leaves—and then a patch of darkness that swallowed it whole. "First Watch," Rand said as the others gathered around. "Two of you range up and down the gully; two more climb up on top, one on either side. The rest of you in the cave. There's a natural vent, and no one will see the smoke in the darkness, so, until daylight, we can have a fire."

That earned him a whispered cheer that made him smile. Tara led the way into the cave. After a few moments of chaotic flashes and shadows, as each Free Forcer pulled out his or her own flashlight, Tara lit a camp lantern, and a soft yellow light filled the cavern.

Rand looked around with satisfaction as his troops quickly and quietly went about the making of a cavern-camp, bringing in wood and water, spreading out their bedrolls, laying out rations. They kept talking to a minimum, as per orders; he had no reason to think anyone would be ranging these forests at night, but one hunter with a radio could have Groundforcers on their tails at first light. He hadn't evaded Artega for so many years by being careless.

Two Forcers came in with shovels in hand and nodded to him. He nodded back and crawled out into the dark to use the latrine pit they had dug. When he finished, he glanced up at the star-studded sky as he turned to go back inside...and froze.

Something flared there that was no star, something with a slow sideways drift, growing rapidly brighter. For a moment, he couldn't make sense of it, then he realized it must be a meteor, not streaking across the sky but instead streaking straight for him. He felt an unreasoning urge to run, though the thing must be tens of kilometres up in the atmosphere, but then the sideways drift suddenly accelerated, and the object *was* streaking across the sky, trailing sparks. He could hear it, too, roaring and crackling. His sense of perspective took another jump; it wasn't tens of kilometres away, it was only four or five kilometres away, and it was going to hit that upthrust bit of mountain he could see outlined against the stars...

Before he could even begin to think about what kind of blast might follow such an impact, the roaring changed pitch, the sparks vanished, and though he heard the meteor strike the mountain, there was no blast: only a strange white glow that slowly faded away.

He glanced at the cave. No one in there could have heard a thing. But the sentries...

As if reading his mind, Vik suddenly materialized at his elbow. "What was that?" the boy said breathlessly, sounding interested and excited for the first time in a long time. *Since his mother died*, the thought repeated uselessly.

"I don't know," Rand said. He put his hand on his son's shoulder. The last time he'd tried that, Vik had pulled away; this time, he didn't, all his attention on the peak where the object had struck—or *landed*—now once again just an obsidian cutout against the twinkling stars. "But tomorrow, we're going to find out."

IN THE FIRST GREY LIGHT, still long before dawn, Rand led the Free Forcers at a forced-march pace toward the mountain, coldly aware that Skandar would have tracked the object's descent and notified Artega. That meant Forcers would already be on their way. Groundforcers couldn't make it for hours yet, but Skyforce would surely be over the site as soon as it was light enough to photograph, and Rand hated having his picture taken...especially by Artega.

Good intentions counted for nothing in the face of near-sheer cliffs and shale-strewn slopes. The sun was already peeking through the low clouds hanging over the distant, just-visible ocean, when at last the Free Forcers could see what had streaked down from space the night before.

"That's no meteorite," breathed Vik, standing at his father's elbow, echoing Rand's thoughts.

Whatever it was had left a scorched mark on the slope a good five hundred metres uphill, then apparently slid and tumbled down it. Now it lay jammed between two huge boulders, a silvery, dented oval about nine metres long and four metres in diameter. Along the path of its slide down the mountain lay strewn bits of fins, antennae, and other, more anonymous, metallic debris. "Tara..." Rand began, turning to his second-in-command.

"On it," she said. "Starax! Ilkor! Mac! Kopec! You're with me. I want every bit of metal small enough to carry off this hillside before the sun clears the ocean. Move!"

They moved, scurrying up the slope. Vik glanced up at Rand, his eagerness to run to the strange object written not only on his face but in every line of his body, but Rand shook his head. "We approach slowly," he said. "That thing could be a weapon, for all we know." Which meant, of course, that as commander, he really should send someone else to investigate for him, but proper procedure be damned.

Whatever there was to be found, he intended to be the one to find it.

Step by step, they moved across the slope, picking their way through shale, until finally, they stood in front of the object. A faint, acrid scent hung around it, and a pale greenish fluid had formed puddles beneath it, but it seemed dormant. Now that they were closer, Rand could see two sliding doors, about two metres long, open two or three centimetres. He edged closer, trying to see through the crack...

...and then jumped back, hearing rifles snap up all around him, as two sets of fingers suddenly emerged through the crack, gripped the sides, and began to pull the doors open.

MELODAN WOKE as the protective gel drained from her face. For a moment, choking on fetid air and finding her head lower than her feet, she struggled frantically against the restraining webbing; then, as the surge of terror subsided, realized she must have landed.

The lid will come off when the last of the gel drains, she reassured herself; but the stuff was almost gone, leaving behind a faint smell of decomposing roses, and the padded panel inches from her nose had not moved.

The manual control, Melodan thought. She felt for and found a short metal level by her right hand and jerked it sharply.

It didn't budge.

She pulled harder, and her heart leaped as something snapped and a crack of night sky appeared—but stopped growing when only an inch wide.

Through that narrow space, she saw a tall spear of rock silhouetted against bright stars. A twisted bit of metal protruding from her left attested to the violence of her landing. The cocoon had saved her—but maybe only temporarily. The automatic and manual releases had both failed, and there was no third alternative.

You really screwed up, didn't you? she thought bitterly. *Asleep when you popped out of dimspace right in front of a Preceptorate cruiser. No escape jump programmed. And now you're going to starve to death in a ready-made coffin.*

Rage filled her. No, she was *not*! That would be the final screw-up, and she wouldn't give her father the satisfaction of saying, "I told you so!"

She began a silent, desperate struggle to raise her right arm to her chest. There were only a few centimetres between her body and the narrow opening to the outside world, but by keeping her arm tight against her body and tugging and scraping her hand from thigh to stomach to breast, fighting the sucking grasp of the damp fabric enveloping her, she succeeded in getting her fingers into the cool night air.

Halfway there, she thought and repeated the struggle with her left hand. By the time those fingers, too, were outside, she was panting, and the smell of her own sweat mingled sharply with the stench of the gel. But she paused only a moment before seizing the edges of the lid and trying to pull them apart.

The metal panels dug into her hands like dull knives. Her fingers tingled, then numbed—but still, she pulled, gritting her teeth.

It was no good. The doors wouldn't budge, and her strength was fading. She pulled her fingers back inside the cocoon and stared bitterly up into the night sky through the crack, feeling the icy air of freedom seeping down around her wet body but unable to reach it.

Somewhere up there was home, and Melodan wished she had never left it. *Maybe Father was right*, she thought. *If I'd listened to him, I'd still be on Newhope, helping Mom and Angela run the ranch. I could be riding Jojo through Painted Canyon right now instead of lying in a coffin on a mountainside a thousand light-years away.*

Home. She remembered crisp autumn air, frost on the golden thunderpines, the smell of bacon drifting up the stairs to her room under the eaves, her mother's sweet soprano mingling with the chords of the synthilyre on Winterfest Eve in the den with its long black beams and grey stone walls.

She could see her father, too, seated on the overstuffed couch, legs crossed comfortably on the opalwood drink table, whittling some small animal out of a piece of foamfir while telling stories of his famous battles, of Deux Roches and Caliban and snowy Baffinbree, orange firelight gleaming in his salt-and-pepper hair, his voice slow and deep and his tone offhand as he spoke of deadly dogfights and hair's-breadth escapes, but his blue eyes bright with adventure.

Melodan always followed him around the ranch as he chopped wood or mended fences, chores he insisted on doing, to the distress of the robots. "A man should keep in touch with what he's fighting for, Melodan," he told her once. "It's too easy to fly and fight just to be flying and fighting, and then you're no better off than one of the Preceptorate's soldierserfs."

Yet sometimes within a week, sometimes within two, always within a month, he was back on active duty, flying and fighting. How many times had she shivered in the pre-dawn cold, her mother's arm around her shoulders, and watched her father climb into the shuttle, always waving and giving her a thumbs-up sign before the hatch hid him? She would crane her neck to catch the last tiny flicker of flame that marked his ascent, long after everyone else had lost sight of it, promising herself that someday he wouldn't leave her behind—someday she'd follow him.

Only to find he didn't want her to.

She closed her eyes to shut out the accusing stars.

SHE WOKE TO DAWN LIGHT, hunger...and the sound of *something* on the rocks outside, crunchings and clickings that her mind was only too willing to give a purely imaginary but nonetheless horrifying chitinous shape.

She clenched her teeth. She would *not* end her days as a box lunch for some nameless monster on an alien mountain-side. She thrust her fingers up into the light, pulled against the doors with all of her strength, sparing nothing this time, ignoring the pain in both hands and muscles...and suddenly something snapped—*not* a bone, though it wouldn't have surprised her—and with a grating whir, the lid of the cocoon slid all the way open.

Melodan sat up painfully, joints creaking, shivering in freezing mountain air—and found herself staring into the muzzle of a rifle.

Peripherally she saw other rifles encircling her, as well as forested foothills, a distant golden plain and even more distant ocean, the red ball of the rising sun, and a great deal of black rock, but the gaping barrel only centimetres from her cold nose rather held her attention. She lay perfectly still while her eyes slowly travelled up the white (white?) barrel to the green-clad man behind it and finally to his black-bearded face and blue eyes. Looking over his shoulder, also holding a rifle, was a boy of maybe seventeen, Standard, his eyes, blue as the bearded man's, wide in his lean brown face, though his gun was aimed as steadily as any of them.

When no one spoke, Melodan finally cleared her throat and said huskily, "Either shoot me or give me a blanket. I'm freezing." Her words formed silvery clouds in the chill air.

"Vik," said the bearded man, and the youngster shouldered his rifle, unshouldered his pack, and drew out a dark-green blanket. Melodan took it gratefully and wrapped it around herself. "Thank you." Keeping a close eye on the guns, she stood, groaning involuntarily, every muscle objecting to the outrageous notion of movement.

"Who are you?" asked the boy.

Melodan glanced at him, then at the older man. "Are you the one in charge?"

"My son asked you a question," he growled.

Melodan looked around at the wreckage-strewn slope, seeing for the first time the long flame-licked and metal-strewn trail her lifeslip had left from the peak to the boulders that had blocked its further descent. "I guess you've realized I'm not from around here."

"Answer the question!"

Melodan tried to shake off the strange feeling of unreality that gripped her. *This isn't a training exercise,* she thought. *This is real. It's part of your mission. Don't mess this up, too.*

She tried to stand at attention. "I am Pilot First Class

Melodan Castille of the Revolutionary Space Force," she said. "I'm here to reopen this planet to the galaxy." *If the Preceptorate hasn't beaten me to it*, she thought, as her discoverers exchanged startled glances.

Then she thought, *What's that buzzing?*

RAND STARED AT THE SLIGHT, sodden girl wrapped in Vik's blanket and didn't have a clue what to say or do next. Her claim was too immense, too absurd—and yet impossible to dismiss, considering the circumstances under which they'd found her. He could see only two possibilities: either she was telling the truth, at least about having arrived from space, or this whole thing had been elaborately stage-managed by Skandar to draw the Free Forcers out of hiding...

...which it had done.

A sound he knew only too well penetrated his consciousness. His head snapped up: out above the plain, three black specks grew rapidly larger.

Skyforcers!

"Take cover!" he shouted. As the Free Forcers scattered like startled birds among the rocks, he grabbed Melodan's arm and pulled her out of the wrecked vehicle and down between the boulders. Vik crouched down beside them, his rifle and his eyes glued skyward. "Starax!" Rand shouted.

"On it, sir!" the Free Forcer shouted, and indeed Rand could see him, crouched down behind a dangerously small rock, assembling a long black tube from three separate parts.

"What's going on?" Melodan asked.

Skyforce answered her before Rand had the chance to.

The buzzing swelled to a roar and a rattle, and a twin line of explosions cracked across the spire of rock and ripped holes in the shattered lifeslip. Shrapnel whined among the boulders. Something stung Rand's cheek; he wiped the back of his hand across the place, and it came away red.

A grey biplane roared over. Rifles, Vik's among them, spat useless fire at it. A second biplane followed hard on its tail. Another explosion bombarded them with rocks and dirt, and acrid smoke burned Rand's nostrils. "Starax!" he shouted again.

"Next pass, sir!"

"Here it comes!" cried Vik.

Lower than the others, a third plane howled toward them, guns blasting across the stone. Rand's heart lurched as a Free Forcer—he couldn't see who—screamed, but then Starax rose from hiding, the rocket launcher on his shoulder. He fired, the missile riding hissing flame straight into the belly of the biplane. It exploded in a ball of yellow fire that slammed into the mountain. Starax jammed another missile into the launcher, but the two remaining aircraft banked and fled.

"Watch her!" Rand ordered Vik and scrambled from cover, running with the others to the spot where the scream had originated. He pushed through the ring of Free Forcers, already certain what he would see, something he had seen far too often: one of his followers sprawled in the ignominious pose of death.

Blood soaked the man's shirt and pooled among the rocks. Rand turned the body over. *Kopec.* He'd escaped from a tek farm just six months earlier, followed the tenuous trail of clues and rumours they had spread across Skandar to one of the places where they periodically met new recruits. All he'd wanted was a little freedom.

All he'd found was a bloody death.

Rand closed Kopec's eyes and straightened, feeling very old.

Tara stepped forward. "I'll arrange a burial party, sir..."

"No."

"Sir?" Tara stared at him.

Rand hardened his heart and his voice. "We don't have time for that. Strip him and put him in the space vessel. If that girl is telling the truth, we can't let Artega have her. Maybe if he has a body to go with the wreckage, he won't look for her—at least for a while."

Tara looked down at Kopec. "I don't like leaving one of our own to that—"

"That's an order, Sergeant!" Rand said, command-snap in his voice.

Tara stiffened. "Yes, sir!" She spun and started stabbing a finger at the other Forcers. "You, you, you and you. You heard the colonel. Strip him and put him into the wreckage."

"The rest of you spread out and pick up all the metal you can," Rand said. "We move out in fifteen minutes; we still have a mission to accomplish. And I don't want so much as a twig broken. We leave no trail for Groundforce. Understood?"

They nodded.

"Do it."

As his troops followed their orders, he returned to the girl, a most un-command-like fury seething in his heart. Kopec would still be alive if she hadn't crashed on this mountain. Ridiculous to blame her...but true, nevertheless. He needed time to cool down before he talked to her. "I can't deal with you now," he snapped at her. "Vik, we're moving out. Watch her. If she tries to run away, shoot her."

He spun on his heel and strode after his troops.

Tor barely heard the voice of the Flight Leader in his headphones, yelling at the control tower, telling them what had happened at the mountain. His hand gripped the joystick so tightly his knuckles were white and his fingers ached, but he barely noticed that, either.

All he could see was that ball of yellow fire slamming into the mountainside, all he could hear was Parl's last, terrified scream as he saw the missile racing toward his plane—that scream, and then the awful silence that had followed it.

Parl, dead. Burned, blasted, scattered in bloody pieces across the cold black rock. Parl, who had befriended him when he'd first arrived at Skybase, who'd trained with him, roomed with him, drunk with him. Parl, shot down by a ragtag bunch of terrorists.

Damn them. Damn them. *Damn* them! They would pay.

He'd see to it.

They would *pay*.

MELODAN STARED AFTER RAND. "SOME WELCOME," she muttered. "Rifles, people dropping bombs on me, and now a threat of summary execution. Nice."

She still couldn't believe what she'd seen. Biplanes! Not just biplanes, but wood-and-fabric biplanes, like something out of Earth's ancient history, when humans first started to fly...a period that had always fascinated her, when the basic techniques of fighting in atmospheric aircraft were first established, techniques that persisted even with spaceplanes.

But even on Earth, the early planes' skins of fabric and frames of wood had soon given way to metal. Why had such an ancient mode of construction been resurrected here?

The boy, Vik, continued to watch her intently, rifle steadily aimed at her heart. Uncomfortable under his steady blue gaze, Melodan wrapped the blanket a bit more tightly around her shoulders. Her eyes wandered to where the four soldiers were stripping their dead comrade of his clothing. As they hosted his naked, blood-soaked body onto their shoulders, she swallowed and looked away, at the sky, at the ground, at anything except *that*—and her glance fell on Vik's weapon. "Why—it's not metal!" she blurted.

"Of course not," Vik said. "It's plastic and ceramic. Who would use metal for..." His voice trailed off as he looked past her at the metal hull of the lifeslip. "Are you really from space?"

"Where else?"

"Another province, maybe...except if another province had something like this, it wouldn't bother with the Battle-field; it would attack Skandar directly."

"Battlefield?"

Vik closed his mouth firmly. Melodan sighed. *Everything I know about this planet is out of date,* she thought. *Who are these people? And who*—she looked out over the plain, where the biplanes had disappeared—*were* they? "Skyforce," Rand had yelled as they'd attacked. She'd also heard him say something about "Groundforce." His own troops seemed to be rebels of some sort. But against whom? Who controlled this planet?

After being jumped by a Preceptorate ship at the dimspace nexus, she wouldn't have been surprised to find platoons of soldierserfs under skies aswarm with the Precep-torate's black Swordcraft. But biplanes—with *propellers?*

The four rebels brought the dead man right past her. Someone had staunched the gaping hole in his chest with his uniform shirt, presumably to keep him from dripping a trail of blood onto the rocks that would make it clear to anyone with half a brain that he hadn't been the original passenger of the lifeslip, but blood still seemed to cover every inch of his body, and blood stained the hands and uniforms of the Free Forcers carrying him. The woman holding his left leg gave Melodan a burning look of hatred as they passed, and Melodan closed her eyes and lowered her head.

Nothing was as it should have been. Avalon was not a quiet backwater. The Preceptorate, if not in actual control, was in the system. And through her stupidity, she'd so far lost her ship, barely survived a crash landing, and come within a hair of getting her head blown off in some local conflict she knew nothing about...and indirectly caused the death of a man she'd never even met, a man whose lifeless body was now being lowered into the compartment that should by rights, by her own stupidity, have been her coffin, not his.

She was in a tailspin, and the ground was coming up fast.

Rand returned, bearded face still as grim as death. He walked past her without so much as a glance, inspected the body that had taken Melodan's place, nodded sharply to the four Free Forcers who had placed it, and then returned to Melodan and glared down at her. "I'm Colonel Rand. I command the Free Forcers."

Melodan started to reply, but he cut her off.

"Not now. Later, I want answers. For now, this is all you have to know: whoever you are, wherever you're from, you're under my orders. Cause trouble, I'll have you bound and gagged—or shot. Understood?"

Melodan felt the flush of her anger in her cheeks but held her temper and simply nodded.

"Good. We're moving out. You've got two minutes to retrieve anything you want from the wreck. And keep that blanket wrapped around you: that blue jumpsuit must be visible for miles."

He turned and strode away, up the slope where the rest of the soldiers seemed to be scouring the rocks for pieces of the wreckage. Melodan looked at the wreck, then at Vik, who nodded. "Go ahead."

He stood and watched her, rifle no longer aimed at her but not exactly aimed away, either, as she climbed back up to where she could see into the passenger compartment. The dead man's eyes were closed; for that, she was grateful. It was bad enough that she had to reach in past his thigh to activate the access panel for the lifeslip's survival kit, her fingers unavoidably brushing against his cold skin: she didn't think she could have done it at all if he'd been staring accusingly at her from clouded eyes.

She found the button she was searching for and pressed it. Something whirred, and she withdrew her hand delicately, then raised up to look expectantly at the panel, just to the right of the passenger compartment.

Just like the doors of the personnel compartment, the access panel stuck after opening only a crack. Melodan swore and tried to pry it open. It moved grudgingly apart another few centimetres, then stuck for good. She stood up, the blanket falling away, and turned to Vik. "I need a crowbar! Can you—"

"No!" That was Rand, cutting off the boy's reply. "Your two minutes are up. We're moving out now."

"But I need my survival—"

"Vik, get her."

"Yes, sir."

Melodan bit off a hot retort. She needed these "Free Forcers," whoever they were, and she had no doubt Rand would have her dragged if she didn't come willingly. "No need," she said grudgingly. "I'm coming."

The panel was open just enough for her to get her hand

through it up to the wrist. She reached in and felt around; her fingers closed on a slim metal case, all she could find, and she pulled it out, slid it into the thigh pocket of her jumpsuit without even looking at it, then snatched up her blanket and walked up to Vik...

...and right past him, and Rand, too. "Come on, Colonel Rand," she said. "We're moving out."

She felt perverse satisfaction when Vik had to run to catch up.

RAND HELD his temper with difficulty as Melodan sashayed past him. The girl was trouble, he could feel it...but she might also be an opportunity. Whatever she was, they couldn't leave her for the Groundforcers who must already be on their way or the Skyforcers who could be overhead any minute. She didn't get far ahead, anyway. Tara grabbed her and, none too gently, shoved her back to Vik, who took her arm firmly. He wouldn't let go again, Rand knew. His son had the tenacity of a bulldog when he'd made up his mind to do something or believe something.

Like his belief that his father was to blame for his mother's death.

Rand led his remaining troops in among the blue-green, spiky trees of the forest. A branch snapped as he pushed it aside, spraying his fingers with dark sap that stung slightly and smelled like cloves. Irritated at himself, he rubbed his hand on his pant leg. *Why not just leave Groundforce a note, telling them which way we went?*

He stiffened as a faint drone reached his ears: Skyforce,

back already—and this time, no doubt, in force. "Double time," he snapped over his shoulder, and after that, there was no time to think about anything but one foot after the other, breathing deep and leaving as little trail as possible.

Twice he led them across large patches of shale, changing direction sharply within each patch, and once they waded along a stream for half a mile, leaving the shallow, icy water only where it flowed between gravelled banks. In the forest, he avoided soft ground—and broke no more branches.

More than two hours after leaving the crash site, they reached a place where the trees thinned and pale rock gleamed in the warm morning sunshine. Rand cocked his head, listening; he heard nothing.

He looked over his shoulder. "Two at a time, every two minutes. Go!"

Immediately, two Free Forcers dashed across the bare shelf of rock, dropping over its far edge.

Rand waited; then, "Go," he said again, and two more followed.

Finally, only Melodan, Vik, Tara, and he were left. Rand motioned Melodan and Vik forward. "Go!"

They were halfway across the rock when Rand heard a buzzing roar, rapidly nearing. He swore as Melodan stopped and looked up, but Vik jerked her down and practically dragged her over the lip of the rock shelf. At the same instant, a Skyforce plane raced over. Rand held his breath, but it didn't circle back. He shook his head. This girl, whoever she was, might very well get them all killed.

With Tara, he dashed across the bare rock and dropped into the shadows on the other side. A narrow path zigzagged down to a black hole, another of their best camping caves.

Some days, Rand would almost be willing to risk detection for the pleasure of sleeping somewhere other than a cave. Not tonight, not after Kopec's death.

Inside, he took a deep breath and looked around. The camp was already taking shape, the orange light of two lanterns reflecting from the damp walls and the stalactites hanging from the high ceiling overhead. The cave continued to an unknown depth—they'd never penetrated past this first large chamber. If the day ever came he could lay aside his gun, Rand wanted to come back and explore it with Vik.

"Good work," Rand told them all. "We move out at dark."

"Then the mission is still on?" Tara said intently. Trust her; nothing mattered more to her than the chance to strike at Skandar. But this time, he agreed with her. They'd put in too much time and effort, risked too much, to call off their plans now. And if Groundforce did pick up their trail back at the mountain, better that they be headed away from the home they had to keep secret at all cost.

"Of course, the mission is still on," he said and deliberately assayed a fierce grin. "We'll see if the Strator can still keep us a secret after tomorrow!"

The Free Forcers cheered. Melodan, sitting by Vik, looked from them to Rand. He took a deep breath and crossed over to her. It was time to get answers. "Now, girl. Where did you come from, and why?"

<hr>

MELODAN RUBBED HER ARM, bruised when Vik had dragged her over the ledge—not that she blamed him; she would have done the same herself if their situation had been reversed. She'd almost gotten her head blown off—again. And she still didn't know *why*. She needed answers—but obviously, Rand wanted them first.

So, she told her story, ignoring Rand's openly skeptical expression. "The Revolution is what cut Avalon off from the Preceptorate," she finished. "But the Preceptorate is back. I was shot down by a Preceptorate cruiser when I entered the system. When the Revolutionary Space Force finds out, you're going to be in the middle of the war."

"We're already in a war," Vik said.

Melodan turned to him. "With *who?*"

But Rand shook his head slightly, and Vik frowned and leaned back against the wall, shadows hiding his face.

Rand ran a hand through his grey-flecked hair. "You say the Preceptorate withdrew from this part of the galaxy more than a century ago. You're wrong." He jabbed a finger at her. "It never left. You just locked it up here—not just the lords and ladies, but the workers, the teks. And nothing has changed! The nobles still live at ease, while teks do all the work and die on their precious Battlefield. God forbid they should face the inconvenience of a *real* war." His face crinkled in a smile that had nothing to do with amusement. "That's where we come in—the Free Forcers. We're giving them a real war." The fierce smile fell away. "We're fighting the Preceptorate. Just like you claim to be. But where has your precious Revolution been for *us* all these years?"

Melodan remained silent for a moment. "The early rebels did what they had to," she said finally. "Their resources were limited. This planet was just a resort for nobles, strategically unimportant. They had no reason to take it. Instead, they just cut it off and left it to die."

"I see. So, you've been fighting to free everyone from the grip of the Preceptorate—everyone except *us*," Rand snarled. "Even to you, the teks of Avalon are worthless."

"That's not true," Melodan protested. "We just...forgot about you. It was a long time ago."

"And now you've remembered us, so your precious Revolutionary Space Force sent *you*? A single rookie pilot? How are *you* supposed to be able to help us free ourselves from the Preceptorate?"

"It was a simple recon mission," Melodan said. "I wasn't supposed to have to fight anyone. I was just supposed to find out what the situation was on Avalon and report back. But the Preceptorate—"

"And now that you know the situation, what will you do?"

Melodan said nothing. That was the crucial question, wasn't it? What would she do? What *could* she do?

"When all else fails, remember your orders," ran a cynical saying among pilots. Her orders were to scout out Avalon and report back.

"I've got to get a message to the RSF," she said slowly. "Those are my orders. There must be communications equipment in the city, probably at the spaceport." She sat up suddenly. "If you can help me get there...there's only one Preceptorate ship in the system now, but more are probably coming. If we can get a message to the RSF, they can lay an ambush!"

"Help you get into the spaceport?" Rand glared at her. "Do you have any idea what you're asking? The old spaceport is now the Skyforce Command Base. It would take an army to mount an assault on it."

"But you *have* an army," Melodan insisted. "How many Free Forcers are there?"

Rand's face closed, and he got angrily to his feet. "You'd have me throw away my entire force to get *you* into the spaceport? You haven't earned the right to ask that of me, girl. I doubt you ever will, even *if* you're telling the truth."

Melodan stiffened. "I haven't lied to you."

"Maybe not. But I haven't survived fifteen years of dodging and fighting the Strator by being trusting. Vik, watch her." Rand went farther back into the cave and started talking to a young woman in a low voice.

Melodan turned on Vik. "What about you?" she demanded. "Do *you* believe me?"

He didn't reply, and she couldn't see his face.

She sat back against the damp stone with a thump, banging her head. Rubbing it with one hand, she seethed. Her "easy" mission had become a nightmare. A corner of the old Preceptorate survived here, and the last remnant of the present Preceptorate had found it. But why? What interest could the Preceptorate have here that could justify them withdrawing a battle cruiser from their defence of Earth?

Unless they had plans to fortify this system, too. And if so...

Then maybe Earth wasn't meant to be the Preceptor's last stand, after all. Maybe Avalon was.

Somehow, she had to get word to the rebels before they expended their resources trying to reduce Earth, unaware that yet another bloody battle awaited them. But she was grounded, through her own idiocy, with no hope of anyone coming after her for weeks or months—if ever. And her only potential allies...

She looked at the shadowy figures seated around the cave. *With allies like these,* she thought bitterly, *who needs the Preceptorate?*

6 / PUNISHMENT

"S*OUTH*?" Artega glared at the young Groundforce lieutenant whose pale face filled the desktop vidscreen. "Are you sure?"

"Yes, Strator. However—" His voice cracked and he cleared his throat. "However, the trail is very faint. Only the dogs have enabled us to follow them as far as we have—and now the trail has crossed onto a large patch of shale where the dogs are useless. We'll have to circle it. It will take some time."

"How much time?"

Sweat beaded the lieutenant's forehead. "A day, more or less, Strator."

"Make it less, Lieutenant."

"Yes, Strator."

"Dismissed." The young man's image vanished, replaced by the latest production figures from the Bubbling Lake clay quarry. The Strator drummed his fingers on the arm of his chair. The Free Forcers' base *couldn't* be south of the crash site—the main road east from Skandar into the mountains and eventually to the Battlefield passed by only thirty kilometres south of where the spacecraft had gone down. So, what were they after? "Skandar."

"Yes, Strator?"

"Are any Battlefield supply shipments scheduled to travel the east road within the next three days?"

"No, Strator."

"Will *anything* be travelling the east road within that time?"

A pause. "Lady Moldar will be moving to her estate in the high mountains tomorrow."

The Strator's fingers stopped drumming. "Anything else?"

"No, Strator."

"So." *That's it, then,* he thought. *That's their target.* He tapped his desktop again and the screen lit with the lieutenant's face once more.

"Yes, Strator?"

"Lieutenant, I want you to call off your trackers."

"Sir?"

"You heard me. Call them off and move south to the east road. Lady Moldar will be moving into the mountains tomorrow. I think the Free Forcers plan to attack her caravan."

"We'll stop them, Strator!"

Artega sighed. "No, you won't. You will allow them to raid the caravan and depart safely—and then you will follow them, taking care to be unobserved. Understood?"

The lieutenant looked troubled. "But Strator, Lady Moldar—"

"*Understood?*"

The lieutenant paled. "Yes, Strator."

"Good. Dismissed." As the young officer's face faded again, Artega allowed himself a small smile before turning to other matters. "Skandar, repeat analysis of the crashed object."

"Yes, Strator." A pause. "Although somewhat different in specific design from those in my database, it appears to be a one-person lifeslip, ejected from a larger space vessel. It was severely damaged upon landing; little can be salvaged from it except its metal."

"And the body found inside?"

"No final conclusion can be drawn until the corpse is returned to the city for autopsy, but visual scanning reveals injuries that could not have been caused by the crash, specifically several bullet wounds. It is possible, however, that he survived the crash, then was killed by the Free Forcers, or when Skyforce attacked the Free Forcers."

"It's possible." Artega keyed a control on his desk and three giant vidscreens extruded from the ceiling. Each lit with pictures of the crash site. "It's also possible the Free Forcers have whoever really rode that thing down."

"I have no data on which to perform probability analysis," Skandar advised him.

Artega ignored the computer. He didn't have any hard data either—but he had something the artificial intelligence would never have: a gut feeling. The Free Forcers had made contact with the pilot of the Revolution scoutship Baron Markus had destroyed eleven days ago. Somehow, the lifeslip had escaped detection and made it to Avalon.

He'd hoped to nab the pilot himself, to offer him in trade to Markus for the space-based support he needed to track down and destroy the Free Forcers once for all. But the fact the Free Forcers had that pilot might be enough to convince Markus to see reason anyway. "Skandar, contact the *Bloodline*."

"Yes, Strator."

A few minutes later Markus was glaring at him from the vidscreen as he made his report. "Why didn't you notify me immediately of this lifeslip?" the baron demanded.

"Skandar has only now confirmed that it *was* a lifeslip," Artega snapped back. "It could have been a weapon from one of the other cities, gone astray from the Battlefield. Why didn't *you* pick it up on your scanners?"

"An excellent question," Markus snarled. "One I will look into personally."

"I assume I can now count on your support for my efforts to eliminate the Free Forcers?"

The baron's eyes narrowed. "If this is some kind of a trick to force me to help you—"

"I can show you the vidrecords."

"Vidrecords can be altered." The baron waved off further protest. "It doesn't matter. No, Strator, you may *not* count on my support. I'm behind schedule trying to get the space-based elements of the defence system back into working condition prior to activation. This Rebel, if he exists, will have to be your responsibility. Capture him alive, if possible, kill him if you have to. And increase security at your spaceport."

"Of course, he'll try to contact his superiors." Artega considered. "We could destroy the transmitters—"

"No, the Preceptor will need them. Find the pilot instead. At once. As long as he's free he's a threat." Markus smiled slightly. "And one other thing: I think you can rest assured that if the rebels *are* warned, the Preceptor shall have you publicly drawn and quartered...no doubt preceded by me. Perhaps that may provide added incentive."

Without a word, Artega broke the connection.

He wished he could do the same to the baron's neck.

A WEEK HAD PASSED since Kyla had visited Tor at the Skyforce Command Base, a week in which each day dragged by as though bound hand and foot with lead chains. Kyla's duties were not onerous—light cleaning and helping Lady Moldar dress, undress, do her hair, and bathe—and she carried them out without speaking, almost without thinking. Silence, fortunately, was exactly what Lady Moldar wanted in her servants.

Kyla felt as though part of her had been torn out, some vital part that made her think and feel normally. It was almost as though her brother had died.

He might as well have, she thought in one of the rare times her lethargy lifted enough for her to feel anger. *He's become one of* them. *They've turned him into everything he used to hate.*

A couple of days after she visited Tor, the household began preparing for the move to Lady Moldar's mountain estate. Boxes had to be packed, rooms in the house they were leaving dust-sheeted and sealed, food prepared for the journey. A caravan of large wheelers was drawn up on the broad winding drive in front of the mansion, and filled with crates, cases, cushions, and clothes.

Kyla packed and carried and dusted and mopped with

the rest of the household staff, mostly older women who chattered a blue streak with each other but seldom spoke to her, though whether they resented her presence or were just put off by her withdrawn sullenness, she didn't know or care.

But on the night before they were to leave the city, something finally happened to draw her out of her shell of misery.

As usual, she was waiting on the Lady as she ate, standing behind her chair with a decanter of wine, ready to refill the Lady's glass the moment it appeared in danger of emptying. Outside the high arched windows of the dining room the mountains were black cutouts against a blazing red sky, the last vestige of the sun that had already vanished behind the peaks. Kyla, idly glancing that way, saw a sight that stabbed her heart like a dagger of ice: four Skyforce airplanes in diamond formation silhouetted against the bloody sunset, passing smoothly and silently from right to left across the window and out of sight.

Something seemed to break in her heart, some wiry knot that had held the gate of emotion sealed shut. Tears suddenly welled into her eyes and her jaw trembled—and Lady Moldar chose that moment to call for more wine.

Kyla stumbled forward, hardly able to see. Lady Moldar held out her cup without even looking at her, but when Kyla tried to pour, her hands shook so badly that the wine ran over Lady Moldar's hand and down her arm, staining the snow-white sleeve of her gown and puddling on the tapestried carpet.

Lady Moldar screamed, the sound shrill and animal-like, slammed her wine cup down on the table, and grabbed Kyla's wrist. Kyla couldn't help it: she burst into tears and dropped the decanter, which rolled across the carpet, spilling the last of its contents onto the blue-and-red images of aristocratic life embroidered there.

"Crying? I'll give you something to cry about, you clumsy brat!" Lady Moldar shouted. "Hildar! Hildar!"

"Yes, milady?" The household head appeared in the door, taking in the scene without the slightest change in expression.

"Bring me the whip." She turned back to Kyla. "Bare your back, tek!"

"My—milady?" Kyla said, barely able to get the words out. "Milady, please, I'm sorry, my brother—"

"I'll hear none of your excuses. Bare your back!" And when Kyla didn't move, the Lady grabbed her, spun her around, and ripped open her servant's dress down its zippered back. Beneath it she wore a simple white shift; Lady Moldar ripped that down the seams. "Bend over that chair," she ordered.

Kyla obeyed, sobbing openly now, clutching the front of her dress to herself.

Hildar returned. She carried a device about a metre long. The first thirty centimetres or so was the handle, black, with a switch and two little lights, one red, one green. A long flat silvery strip about a centimetre wide stuck out from the handle. At its tip glowed a little red light.

A neural whip. Kyla had seen one used at the tekfarm. It was a last-resort mode of discipline. It wouldn't actually damage her, she knew. There would be no stripes, no blood, no bruising. What there would be...was pain.

She choked back her tears. "Lady Moldar, please, I'm sorry, it was an accident. Please don't—"

"Be quiet, tek!" Lady Moldar flicked the switch on the

handle. The red light glowed; after a moment the green one came on.

"Milady, please—"

"Shall I stay, milady?" Hildar asked, politely.

"Perhaps you'd better, Hildar. This tek may need some help returning to her quarters once I've finished disciplining her."

She advanced on Kyla, who made no more protests. Instead, she closed her eyes, trying to prepare herself for—

She screamed as what felt like liquid fire traced a lingering, excruciating line down her naked back. She could feel it burning, searing through the skin, the muscle, down to the bone, flaying every nerve. She felt something warm flowing down her chin and realized she had bitten her lip; felt something warm flowing down her legs and knew her bladder had let go.

The agony had just begun to fade when she felt the whip again...and again...and...

Mercifully, she passed out.

WHEN SHE CAME TO, she was in her quarters. The pain in her back was gone, but her lip was swollen and sore, every muscle in her body seemed stiff, and she stank of sweat and urine.

She still wore the torn dress and shift; she got up and stripped out of them, then poured herself a hot bath and immersed herself in the steaming water.

She thought of Tor, but she didn't cry again. The pain had leeched the tears out of her. She had lost her brother, but she still had her own life to live, and one thing she knew, with crystal clarity: she would not live it in the service of Lady Moldar.

"I'm going to run away," she murmured, and then repeated, loudly and firmly, so the blue-tiled walls of the bathroom echoed to it, "I'm going to run away!"

Tomorrow they left for the mountain estate.

Tomorrow, she would be free.

"Good-bye, Tor," she whispered.

She went to bed and fell instantly asleep.

MELODAN DOZED as the day wore on but jerked awake from a vivid dream of being shot at by a Preceptorate cruiser. She sat up and stared around. Vik's eyes glinted at her from his shadowed face. "I'm not going to run away," she told him.

"I was ordered to watch you."

"Am I really that interesting?" He didn't reply, and Melodan shook her head. "You're a bit young to be a guerilla, aren't you?"

"Old enough," said the boy.

"To do what?"

"To kill."

Melodan blinked. "Sorry I asked." She shifted position to ease an ache and felt against her leg the hard oblong shape of the locked case she had salvaged from the wreckage. She frowned. What could be in it? Mentally, she listed the lifeslip's supplies—and stiffened. The size, the shape, the security lock—the case contained a blazer!

And unless the lock had been damaged in the crash, she could open it simply by pressing her thumb in the right spot.

She reached for her pocket, then reconsidered and scratched her leg instead. She wasn't sure she wanted the Free Forcers to know she had a blazer—not yet.

As twilight deepened, the Free Forcers gathered their weapons and packs. Rand slipped out for a few minutes. "All clear," he reported upon his return. "But if you hear a plane, dive for cover. Show a light and you'll be digging latrines for a year!" Everyone laughed. "Let's go."

They left the cave in single file, Rand leading, Melodan second, Vik close behind, then the others, and followed the stream downhill, staying in the gully until the high rock walls gave way to forested slopes. Then Rand splashed across the stream and struck off through the trees. He seemed in no doubt about his path despite the darkness and tangled undergrowth, and they hiked almost as fast as during the day. Muscles Melodan had not used since she left the ranch began to burn, but she gritted her teeth and kept pace, noting furiously that Vik wasn't even breathing hard.

Suddenly Rand stopped, so abruptly Melodan walked into him. "Shh!" he said without looking around, then cupped his hands to his mouth and made an unearthly hooting sound. A woman appeared among the trees, wraithlike.

"Hello, Merda," said Rand. "All quiet?"

"Haven't even heard a skreeker. But I was a bit worried about you. A lot of planes up north."

"We were a bit worried, too." Rand paused. "Merda, Kopec's dead. Skyforce." Merda gasped, and Rand put his hand on her shoulder. "I'm sorry." She didn't reply, and after a moment he let his hand fall. "Did you find us a safe campsite?"

"This way," Merda said tightly.

She led them to a clearing in a little hollow surrounded by tall trees. Rand gathered the Free Forcers around him. "No fires, no tents," he instructed. "Usual watches. We don't know when the target will appear, so we'll have to be ready." He paused. "Well, what are you waiting for?"

Murmuring among themselves, the Free Forcers dispersed, spreading blankets around the clearing, except for three who faded away into the trees like Merda. Vik found a couple of blankets for Melodan and lay down near her. She didn't even have time to wonder what tomorrow's "target" was before her exhausted body and mind joined each other in sleep.

MELODAN WOKE to early morning sunlight, cold feet, and voices. Groaning, she rolled over and sat up, joints creaking, feeling as if she'd been beaten with a stick. The top of her thigh was bruised from lying on the blazer case.

Everyone else seemed to be up already, stowing blankets and cleaning weapons. Rand, striding by, stopped and looked down at her. "I should tie you up and gag you until we're done today," he said conversationally, "but I won't. I'll just make sure you're watched every minute and shot if you try to warn the caravan. You'll go with Vik and Tara." He turned and left her.

"Good morning to you, too," she muttered, and struggled to her feet.

At Vik's insistence, she reluctantly parted with her blankets. Everyone else wore warm-looking, if rather shapeless, zippered jackets, but there seemed to be none to spare, and Melodan had to admit it would be hard to push her way through the Avalonian forest while trying to keep a blanket wrapped around her shoulders. She stood shivering and wished the Free Forcers would get their show on the road.

Shortly, they did. They left the clearing and made their way southward, spreading out so that each group of two or three was twenty or thirty metres from the next. After a few minutes, the trees thinned. A moment later they halted at the edge of a broad road paved with pale gravel. It gleamed like silver in the morning light.

"Now what?" she whispered to Vik, earning a glare from Tara.

"We wait," Vik replied. "Silently."

Melodan sat down with her back to a tree and resigned herself to hypothermia. She hated feeling so helpless, so out of control of events. On Earth, the Preceptorate and the Revolutionary Space Force were facing off in one of the last great battles of the century-long struggle. Somewhere near Avalon, a Preceptorate cruiser could be setting up system defences, and the rebels knew nothing of it. Melodan would have given anything to be able to do something about one or the other. Instead, she was unwelcome baggage for a band of guerillas who claimed to be fighting the same enemy as her but didn't believe she was fighting the same enemy as them.

Such gloomy thoughts kept her occupied until the moment a hooting call came from down the road to the right. Vik and Tara scrambled up, and Melodan joined them. "Caravan coming," Vik told her. "Stay out of sight."

Melodan squelched a surge of rebelliousness and

nodded. If she were to get the help she needed from these people, she had to prove they could trust her.

A few minutes later, she heard the rumble of approaching machinery and caught a whiff of burning alcohol, and through a screen of branches watched the first vehicle roll by, trailing dust. It was thirty feet long, an ungainly box set on twenty wheels. White with pink swirls, trimmed with gold along the elaborately carved corners and the many silver-tinted windows, it was the ugliest thing Melodan had ever seen.

It was followed by another, a different colour but just as ugly, then another, and another—and then something exploded to the left, shaking the ground, and all the vehicles ground to a jerking halt, one right in front of Tara and Vik.

A door at the front flew open and an angry man in in a grey uniform jumped down. An instant later, a larger door in the side of the vehicle slid open and from it emerged a young woman about Melodan's age. She had black hair bound up in a sever bun and wore a short white tunic belted with a red sash. She looked both ways along the stalled caravan. "What's wrong?" she called to the grey-clad man.

"Some problem up front," he said. "I'll go—"

"You will stand very still and raise your hands above your heads," said Tara, emerging from the trees with her rifle pointed at them both.

The girl gaped at her, but the driver stepped forward angrily. "Do you know who—"

Tara's gun cracked and Melodan jumped. Dust spurted from the ground by the driver's right foot. He stared down at the miniature crater that had appeared there. "The next one will be higher," said Tara coldly. "Vik!"

Vik stepped into the open. "Easy pickings," he said conversationally. He glanced up and down the road. "Not a Forcer in sight."

"What's going on?" demanded a new voice, and a tiny woman appeared in the doorway of the vehicle. Dressed in flowing pink, with rings glittering on every finger and a diamond tiara blazing in the elaborate swirl of her grey-streaked black hair, she was obviously, Melodan thought, Someone Important.

But Vik brushed past her without a second glance. Someone screamed as he entered the vehicle, but he snapped "quiet!" and got it.

"Who are you?" the woman said furiously. "What other province dares—?"

"No other province, Lady Moldar," said Tara. "We don't fit into your neat little world of nobles and Forcers and teks. We're just people—free people."

"You're teks," the Lady snapped. "No noble would—"

"Would what? Steal?" Tara's voice was bitter. "You've stolen the labour and lives of thousands of teks for decades!"

"How dare you—"

Tara's rifle jerked upward and Melodan stiffened. But the Free Forcer didn't fire—quite. "Shut up," she said. The Lady reddened but had the sense to obey.

Vik emerged with his backpack bulging. "Done!"

The girl in the white tunic stared at him again as he went past her.

"Anything besides the electronics?" asked Tara.

"Food." He held up a jar that glistened wetly. "Candied spiderfish eggs, anyone?"

Tara shuddered. Further back in the trees, so did Melodan. Vik, laughing, turned and smashed the jar against the vehicle's polished wooden side. The eggs made a blue-black stain that oozed slowly to the ground, and the outraged Lady suddenly found her voice again.

"You won't get away with this! The Forcers will—"

"We already *have* gotten away with it, Lady Moldar," Vik said lightly. "Many times."

"Lies! I've never heard..."

"The Strator hasn't exactly been broadcasting the news."

Someone at the head of the caravan shouted and Vik waved. He glanced the other way and apparently received some signal Melodan could not see, for he waved in that direction, too. "Road's blocked both ways," he said. "Time to go."

Tara nodded, and bowed sardonically to the Lady. "I trust the rest of your journey is equally pleasant," she said, and she and Vik re-entered the forest, silently gathered Melodan, and left the caravan behind.

"I'll see you hung!" Lady Moldar shouted after them.

Melodan asked none of the many questions tumbling in her head. Tara, she surmised, might as easily shoot her as answer. Instead, she kept her mouth shut and hoped that now the raid was over she might be able to convince Rand that his next action should be to get her into the spaceport.

The Free Forcers were to rendezvous back at the clearing where they had camped, but Tara, Vik. and Melodan hadn't gone far when Tara stopped. "We're being followed," she said without looking around.

Vik nodded. "You two go on. I'll double back and see who it is."

"Right." Tara glared at Melodan and jerked her head in

the direction they were to go. As they plodded on, Vik vanished.

But seconds later they heard him shout, "Tara!"

At once Tara whirled and dashed back, Melodan close behind. She expected to find that Vik had surprised one of the Lady's bodyguards, or perhaps a Forcer, but the person he held at gunpoint was neither.

Pale but determined, the young girl in the white tunic faced Vik's rifle and met his gaze squarely.

THE MORNING AFTER WHIPPING KYLA, Lady Moldar acted as if the previous evening's punishment had never happened. Kyla helped her get dressed in her chosen travelling garb, a hideous pink confection complete with diamond tiara, then trailed her out to the wheelers. Presumably, she had chosen her ugly outfit to match the equally ugly decor of the wheelers.

Having made up her mind that either along the way or once they reached the mountain estate she would run away, Kyla carried out each of her final duties—packing odds and ends that had been forgotten until just now, once running up four flights of stairs to retrieve a brooch the Lady just had to have—promptly, efficiently, even cheerfully, because she knew that soon she'd be free of such duties forever.

Final preparations had begun before sunup, so despite all the last-minute preparations, the caravan of wheelers rolled off the grounds of the mansion while the day was still young. Inside the caravan she shared with Lady Moldar and Hildar, Kyla sat on a pink-cushioned chair, her feet resting on white shag carpeting, and looked out through darkly tinted windows at the fields, then forests, passing by.

Soon they began to climb, the road snaking back and forth as it mounted the foothills. Trees pressed close to the road's pale gravel. Once, a wheeler loaded with giant logs passed them going the opposite direction. Other than that, they saw no one.

And then, suddenly, they stopped. Lady Moldar sat up, looking annoyed. "Kyla," she snapped, "get out and find out what the problem is."

"Yes, milady," Kyla said, and thought, *Now's my chance.*

But when she jumped out, she found herself faced with a determined-looking young woman in green military fatigues, carrying a rifle that Kyla was on the wrong end of. An even younger man—a boy, really—emerged from the forest as well, and farther back among the trees she glimpsed another young woman.

As Kyla watched the pillaging of the caravan, two emotions boiled inside her: glee that Lady Moldar had finally met her match, and incredulous excitement that here, at last, were the Free Forcers she'd thought nothing but a myth. *I told you, Tor,* she thought. *If we'd fled into the mountains...*

But no. Tor was gone. He was a Skyforcer, now—and enemy to these Free Forcers.

Somehow, she had to join them.

They finished robbing the caravan and disappeared into the forest again. Lady Moldar snapped at Kyla, "Get in! We're going back to Skandar City."

At the head and tail of the line of wheelers, drivers and servants struggled with the heavy branches the Free Forcers had dragged across the road, anxious to get away as quickly as possible from the guns of the Free Forcers the forest suddenly seemed full of. No one was close to her. No one was looking at her, except Lady Moldar.

Without a backward glance at the wheelers, she plunged into the forest.

"Kyla!" she heard Lady Moldar's outraged shrike behind her. "Kyla, you come back this instance or..."

Whatever threat she had to make, Kyla didn't hear, or care to hear. She ran until she tripped and fell, almost gouging an eye out on a branch; then she slowed her pace to a trot, and finally to a walk.

There was no sign of the Free Forcers.

She was lost.

But she'd barely had time to reflect on what that might mean when the Free Forcer boy found her.

RAND WAS PLEASED with the success of the mission; even more pleased because he'd had a message from the scouts he'd sent along their backtrail that the Groundforcers who had arrived at the crash site had given up the chase. Now the Free Forcers rested among the trees by a spring not far from the road...all of them except Tara, Melodan—and Vik.

"They should be here by now," he growled and was about to order scouts out to look for them when, suddenly, there they were—with a girl in tow, wearing the ridiculous short tunic and sash of a noble lady's servant.

Tara had hold of the girl's arm; she almost dragged her up to Rand. "She followed us," Tara said. "But she's clean. No weapons." Tara released her. "Says her name is Kyla."

The girl tilted her chin up and met his gaze squarely. "I want to join you."

"Do you even know who we are?" Rand asked.

"You're the Free Forcers. I've heard of you. Everyone has heard of you."

"The Free Forcers are a myth. Everyone's heard that, too."

"Myths didn't just rob Lady Moldar's caravan." There was something in the way she said the name "Lady Moldar," some undercurrent of hatred, that made Rand think she had plenty of reason for running away.

"True enough," Rand said. "But you realize, if you join us, there's no going back. Myths can't live in normal society." He nodded in the direction of the road. "We could still get you back to the caravan. You could say you thought you'd seen something in the woods we dropped, you went after it, and you fell and hurt your ankle. A believable story. The life of a maidservant in a great lady's house is very different from life out here, Kyla."

"I would rather die than return to that monster."

Rand studied her. She meant it. He nodded. "Well, then, Kyla, welcome to the Free Forcers. Vik!"

"Yes, sir?" said the boy, coming up to him.

"Kyla is joining us. Look after her."

"Yes, sir." He took the girl away, over to where Melodan sat, looking at Rand through narrowed eyes.

He glanced at Tara. "Did Melodan cause any trouble?"

"No, sir." She sounded almost disappointed. "But I still don't trust her."

"You don't trust anybody," Rand said mildly. "You don't trust this tek that's just joined us, either, do you?"

"No, sir," Tara said flatly.

"Good. I wouldn't have it any other way." He nodded in Vik's direction. "I've put Vik in charge of the new girl. Melodan's in your keeping until we get home. Try to avoid shooting her."

Was that a smile? Maybe...barely. "If you insist, sir."

"I do." He raised his voice to the Free Forcers at large. "We're moving out! But tomorrow—tomorrow we'll be home!"

They cheered at that, and for their sakes, Rand kept smiling, but inside, the winter thoughts came crowding.

How could it be home when no one waited there for him? How could it be home without Lissa?

No answers came to him. They never did.

"This is a hobby of yours, isn't it?" Melodan said to Vik, watching Kyla approach.

"What?"

"Collecting strange girls."

He snorted. "My father collects them. I just look after them."

Melodan wanted to walk with Kyla, hoping to learn more about Avalon—maybe even something that would help her accomplish her mission—but Tara took charge of her, and Tara was not about to allow someone she obviously thought of as her prisoner to talk to anyone.

They worked steadily uphill, out of the pass through which the road ran, but circled below the mountain where Melodan had crashed. All of them kept their ears perked for Skyforce, but the only buzzing Melodan heard was that of the tiny, iridescent insects that swarmed around them, biting, as the day grew hot. At first, she swatted at them furiously, but that only soaked her in sweat that attracted more, and finally, she gave up and tried to ignore the creatures like the

Free Forcers did. Gradually, she was able to concentrate on other things, like her sunburned neck, the chafing of her borrowed clothes, the fiery spots on her feet that marked breaking blisters, and the remaining aches from the previous hikes and her unorthodox planetfall.

Their camp that night was cold and cheerless; Rand still would not permit a fire. Melodan gnawed on dried beef and dryer bread and cheese, grudgingly provided by Tara, and promised herself that once they got where they were going, she was going to have it out with Rand. After that, things would be different.

The second day passed like the first. Toward evening, they reached a stream and followed it uphill until rock walls loomed above them, and they were walking along a narrow, mossy ledge above a roaring cataract. Leaden-limbed, Melodan put one aching foot down on a large, flat rock. She barely had time to gasp as it slid into nothingness—then Tara's quick hands pulled her back to safety.

Heart pounding, she managed a weak smile. "Thanks."

Tara's only answer was a scowl and a shove.

The ledge and the gorge gradually broadened, and as the sun slipped out of sight behind them, they emerged all at once into open space, and Melodan gasped.

Hemmed in by tall ramparts of stone to north and south and a high waterfall to the west, the valley before them could only have been seen from directly overhead. Trees and flowering shrubs grew in wild profusion along the stream that wound its length, bounded by lush fields of wheat and corn. Cattle lowed, and a shift in the wind brought the sharp smell of woodsmoke. For a moment, Melodan couldn't see any buildings. Then, people moved in the distance, and suddenly she could pick out heavily camouflaged huts huddled beneath tall trees. If they were this hard to see on the ground, she imagined they were all-but-invisible from the air.

As though their packs had suddenly lightened, the Free Forcers' pace quickened, and they swept Melodan with them into the fields.

As they neared the buildings, a boy cried shrilly, "They're back!", and moments later, a laughing, shouting horde surrounded them—mostly women and children, though Tara was met by a broad-shouldered man who swept her off her feet and planted a kiss on her lips that she returned eagerly.

But no one greeted Vik more than casually, and Melodan watched him until he looked her way and saw her staring. *Where is the rest of his family?* she wondered, turning away. Suddenly lonely amid all the reunions, she glanced at the sky.

And where is mine?

KYLA LOOKED around with wide eyes. She'd never experienced anything like this hubbub of casual friendliness. The tekfarm had been sullen and silent, and Lady Moldar's household had been grim and austere. She had never imagined people acting like this, so open with their emotions and with each other...

...so *free.*

Rand took aside a young, pregnant woman, who suddenly threw her arms around him, sobbing, and Kyla remembered hearing of a man killed by Skyforce the day before the raid on Lady Moldar's caravan. She swallowed and looked away. Death was a constant threat to the Free Forcers...yet, somehow, they managed to put it behind them in this moment of reunion, as if nothing else mattered but the fact that they were together.

She used to feel like that with Tor.

Finally, the entire group, no longer a military unit but just friends and neighbours, continued toward the village, Kyla limping on aching, blistered feet. She'd never walked as far in her life as she had since fleeing the caravan.

More than once, she heard her name in the conversation bubbling around her as curious stay-at-homes were told about her and the mysterious Melodan. She looked at the other girl out of the corner of her eye. Another tek wanting to join the Free Forcers? Kyla didn't think so. A young noble, taken prisoner? What else was there but tek, Free Forcer, or noble?

In a small green space at the centre of the village, Rand held up his hands for silence. "We leave one kind of work for another," he said. "The fields are ripe!" The crowd groaned, and he grinned at them. "But the harvest will wait. Tonight, we celebrate!"

The Free Forcers cheered, then scattered, laughing and talking. Rand took Vik aside and spoke quietly to him. Melodan, free of Tara's grasp, came walking toward Kyla, who felt a rising panic. Had she seen Kyla looking at her? What would she say?

As it turned out, all she said was, "Hi. I'm Melodan Castille." She smiled and held out her hand.

Kyla shook it, smiling back in relief. "I'm Kyla XA2—" She stopped suddenly. Her ID code had been assigned to her by Skandar. She'd never need it again. "Um...Kyla." She shifted on her feet, trying hopelessly to find some way of standing that didn't hurt.

Melodan chuckled. "You, too, huh?"

"I'm not used to walking," Kyla said.

"Me neither. I'd rather be flying. Come on, let's find someplace to sit."

She led the way to a bench at the edge of the village green while Kyla stared at the back of her head. *Flying?* "You're a Skyforcer?" she blurted as she sat down. She didn't think she'd ever done anything that felt as good.

"Uh, no," Melodan said. She hesitated. "Look, you might find this hard to believe..."

"*I* certainly did," Rand said, joining them.

Melodan sighed. "Colonel, we're on the same side."

"Right now, the only 'side' I'm on is that of survival," Rand said. "For the next month, harvest is more important than revolution."

"Colonel, we may not have a month! If that Preceptorate cruiser—"

"If we don't get the harvest in, everyone in this valley will be dead of starvation by spring," Rand said flatly. "That reality takes precedence over any 'ifs' you can bring forward." He looked at Kyla. "We have only one empty hut. I'm afraid you and Melodan will have to share."

Kyla looked at her glowering new roommate. "That will be...fine," she said tentatively.

MELODAN SHOULD HAVE DONE something to put the other girl at ease, but she didn't feel like it. A month, at least, before she could count on any help from the Free Forcers, and no guarantee of it, even then?

If her suspicions were true, if the Preceptor intended to make Avalon his final stronghold, they might not have a month. The assault on Earth must be only days away. The Preceptor could already be on his way.

She had to find a way to change Rand's mind, or she would have no choice but to run away, try to get down to the spaceport and its precious transmitters by herself. But without a guide, without knowing what she might face when she got there...she didn't like her chances.

Lost in her own thoughts, she temporarily forgot about Kyla. When she glanced up again, she saw the girl looking at her uncertainly, as if wondering whether she really wanted to share a hut with such a surly stranger.

Hmmm. Kyla. Kyla came from the city. Maybe *she* could be Melodan's guide if it came to that.

Besides, she could use a friend.

She managed a small smile. "Don't worry," she said. "I don't bite."

Kyla smiled back, tentatively.

The bustle of the Free Forcers transformed itself within an hour into a feast featuring fresh meat brought back that day by hunters. Kyla ate voraciously of what she informed Melodan was "barbecued trillbuck," washing it down with "starberry wine."

The food smelled delicious, but Melodan, sighing, stuck to bread and cheese, washing it down with water. "I'll explain later," she said when Kyla asked her about it. This didn't seem the time or place to try to explain about coming from the stars, much less the fact that, as descendants of long-term colonists, all the Free Forcers had been genetically modified to metabolize the proteins of local life forms, whereas she had to stick to Earth-normal foods or risk starving to death on a full belly. The wheat was Earth wheat, and the cows were Earth cows, so bread and cheese it was.

She did explain it privately to Rand, thinking it might encourage him to trust him, but he just laughed at her. "Very consistent," he said, as he accepted another slice of meat from the Free Forcer tending the spit. "But you don't know what you're missing."

As the celebration waned, Vik guided Melodan and Kyla to the hut they would share on the edge of the village. He had been mostly silent even during the feast, eating almost nothing, though he had drunk rather heavily of the starberry wine. As the three of them walked through the darkness away from the bonfire, Melodan said softly, "No one came to meet you when we got here today, Vik. Don't you have any family besides Rand?"

"My mother is dead," Vik said shortly.

Is that why you've built such a shell around yourself? Melodan wondered. "I'm sorry," she said out loud. "What happened?"

He stopped. "This is your hut," he said, pointing to it. Then he walked away.

Kyla went in at once. Melodan looked after Vik thoughtfully for a moment, then followed her roommate, closing the door on the dying sounds of merriment.

Kʏʟᴀ sᴜʀᴠᴇʏᴇᴅ ʜᴇʀ ɴᴇᴡ ǫᴜᴀʀᴛᴇʀs. The hut was only a single room with mud-and-stone walls and a ceiling of low, unpeeled beams, but it had an enormous fireplace and two wooden beds with straw-filled mattresses that looked comfortable enough; not exactly up to Lady Moldar's standards, but better than she'd had at the tekfarm. Two wooden chairs and a small, round table graced one corner. Candles burned on each end of the mantlepiece.

Someone had built a fire earlier; coals still glowed in the fireplace. Kyla knelt down and built up the blaze again with the pile of wood near the hearth. As the flickering light brightened the hut, she straightened and sat on one of the beds, yawning. Melodan sat on the other.

"If we're going to live together, we should get to know each other," Melodan said. "Where are you from?"

Kyla shrugged. "Nowhere. Just a farm, a long way east of Skandar. What about you?"

"Uh...if you don't know yet, I think I'll save that for a bit."

What was this girl's problem? First, she wanted to talk; then, she didn't. Well, Kyla could be as silent and mysterious as anyone. She lay back on the bed, blinking up at the ceiling. "Fine."

"Any family?" Melodan prompted.

Kyla didn't reply. She might not have replied even if Melodan had been more forthcoming herself. The question stung. *No, I don't have any family...not anymore,* she thought. *Skyforce took it away.*

Melodan sighed. "Fair enough. Why should you talk to me if I won't talk to you?" She took a deep breath. "I'm from the stars."

Kyla thought she'd misunderstood. She raised up on one elbow. "From where?"

"The stars. You know." Melodan pointed up. "Out there."

Kyla stared. Had they roomed her with a lunatic? "That's impossible!"

"That's what Rand thinks." Melodan got up, grabbed the poker from beside the fireplace, and thrust it angrily at the burning wood. Swirling sparks raced up the chimney. Not all the smoke followed suit. Kyla coughed, but the cloying, incense-like fumes of the didn't seem to bother Melodan. She kept poking. "He thinks I'm a spy for Skandar, or maybe from some other province. But it's true. I was sent here to find out what's happened since the starships left." She shook her head. "I found out, all right. A Preceptorate cruiser destroyed my scoutcraft." She sounded bitter. "I bailed out, my lifeslip crashed in these mountains, and the Free Forcers rescued me—or captured me."

Why would she tell such a preposterous story? Kyla wondered. Maybe she'd run away, too, and was still afraid to give out her true identity. Maybe she was a noble and was afraid Rand would hold her for ransom. "I—I don't know what to say."

Melodan sighed and returned the poker to the rack. "You don't believe me. I suppose I can't blame you. But that's my story. What's yours?"

Her own story seemed boring by comparison. But at least it was true. "It's kind of long."

Melodan settled on her bed. "I've got time."

Rand saw Vik come back to the fire and sit down, alone as always, so far from the flames that they barely illuminated his face and he could hardly have felt their heat. For a moment, he felt a flash of anger at his son for continuing to nurse his pain, for clasping it so tightly it cut him off from everything and everyone around him...but the anger passed quickly.

How could he blame his son for something he knew he did himself?

Oh, he had stayed close to the fire, talking and joking with Tara and Starax and the others, listening to the tales of their raid on the caravan grow progressively more outlandish, drinking and eating, the very picture of the down-to-earth commander mingling with his troops.

But inside, his heart was as far from the warmth as Vik's, and for the same reason.

When the fire died, he would trudge his lonely way across the green to his house, the largest in the village, the one he'd built with his own hands when at last the troop he had led from the Battlefield found this hidden place in which to settle and made the decision to bring their families here to live.

It had been remarkably easy to get word to their wives and husbands, parents and siblings and lovers, that they were still alive, that there was a place where they could live free of the Skandar AI and Strator Artega, free of the nobles and the Forcers...or at least as free as a life could be in hiding.

Singly and in pairs, their loved ones had come to them, sneaking out of the city at night, disappearing from tekfarms through mysterious holes in the wire, abandoning the transport wheelers they drove, slipping away unnoticed from construction sites. No one had ever worried about teks running away because there was nowhere for them to go.

Now, there was.

Rand remembered the day Lissa had arrived in the valley, with Vik, little more than a toddler then, riding on the shoulders of one of the Free Forcers escorting them. They were at the head of a straggly train of a dozen or more family members, but they were all Rand could see.

They'd been so happy then, so deliriously happy. He'd carried her across the threshold of the four-room house he had built, afraid she would be horrified when she realized how hard and basic a life they would be living here...but all she had cared about was being with him, and Vik, in a place where they worked for themselves and couldn't be ordered from place to place at the whim of a machine or a noble—and couldn't be ordered to fight and die on the Battlefield.

But the fighting had continued. The Free Forcers' raids caused only minor damage—their numbers were too small, their supplies too scant—but they were carefully chosen to annoy the Strator and the nobles, and even more importantly, to attract the attention of teks. Teks talked to teks. Word got around. Not everyone believed the Free Forcers were real—Artega never acknowledged any of their actions officially—but enough believed that a steady trickle of recruits had come to them over the years.

For a time, that was all Rand had wanted. He thought if he kept his community alive and slowly growing, that was victory enough—as much victory as he could hope for. He knew they couldn't fight the Strator head-on, much as he would have liked to, and except for that slight disappointment, he was content...content, because he had Lissa, and Vik, who grew up into a fine young man.

Within their community, they had many skills. Their children were taught by many teachers, not only those with academic knowledge but those who knew how to carve wood and shape stone and fire pottery...and those who knew how to shoot, to fight, to kill. Vik grew up to be a Free Forcer, as Rand had known he would, as surely Lissa had known he would, as well, though perhaps she had not realized as fully as Rand what that would mean.

"What kind of life will he have?" Lissa whispered to Rand one night in their bed. "Always fighting, hiding...running, if Artega ever finds this place..."

Rand ran his fingers through her long, soft hair, hair that always smelled to him of sunlight, rain, wind, and flowers, all rolled into one. He could have happily breathed in that scent for hours. "At least he's free."

"Oh, Rand." She snuggled her head to his chest, her voice muffled. "He's not free. None of us are free. We've just built ourselves a different prison. Maybe it's a little larger than the prison of being a tek, or a Forcer, but it's still a prison. We're still prisoners of the Strator and Skandar, as long as we have to hide from them."

"I've done all I can," Rand whispered. "There aren't enough of us to overthrow Artega, Lissa. You know that. So many would die...and we'd fail."

"I know." He could hardly hear her. "I know. And that will never change, will it, my love? Nothing will ever change...not even for Vik."

After that, she was silent, but beneath his hands, her body shook.

And a month after that...a month after that, she was dead.

Rand stood up abruptly. Most of the Free Forcers had left the dying fire, except for an older man whispering to his wife, who sat with her head on his shoulder; Tar, still deeply engrossed in soft conversation with Marik, her lover...

...and Vik.

Rand crossed the well-trodden grass to him, half-expecting him to run away. But he stayed put, though he didn't look up as Rand approached.

Rand sat down on the log beside his son. "Vik," he said. "We have to talk. About...Lissa. Your mother."

"What's there to talk about?" Vik said flatly. "She's dead."

"And you blame me for it."

Vik said nothing.

Rand looked at the blood-red glow of the embers. "Of course, you do. Just as I blame myself." He shook his head. "But it's not true, Vik. I didn't kill her. A virus did that."

"A virus," Vik spat. "A virus that would never have killed her in Skandar. If she'd been anywhere else but here, anywhere with proper medical care...but you dragged her out here. You brought her out here, and it killed her." He stood up. "You're right, Dad, I do blame you. And I hate you for it!" He ran into the darkness.

Tara and Marik and the other couple had gone to their huts while they spoke, so there was no one to see as Rand, commander of the Free Forcers, lowered his head into his hands and wept bitter tears.

9 / THE INVITATION

Artega did not grant personal interviews often. But as much as he preferred to conduct business by vidscreen, he could not refuse to see Lady Moldar. Though not a member of the Council, she was a major creditor of three of the Councillors. That gave her power he could not ignore.

Of course, he knew *why* she wanted to see him. As he had anticipated, the Free Forcers had raided her caravan. Groundforce was even now tracking them; he expected a report shortly. But the Strator had no intention of letting Lady Moldar know that.

As the panelled door slid open to admit her, he rose, smiling. "Lady Moldar! Always a pleasure to—"

"I have never been so outraged in my life!" Lady Moldar planted herself across the desk from him, glaring, her anger giving her an effective stature much greater than her diminutive frame. "Teks attacking nobles? Renegade Forcers? Why wasn't I warned? Why wasn't I provided with an escort? What are you doing about those—terrorists?"

Artega kept his smile. "Lady Moldar, the Council felt it

best to keep news of the terrorist activity in the mountains as quiet as possible. They feared it might incite unrest among the teks."

"You let me go up there knowing I could be attacked!"

Yes, milady. "No, milady. Until now, the terrorists have only raided unoccupied estates. The Council did not believe they would dare attack a noble directly."

"And you agreed?"

"Milady, I thought there might be some danger of such an attack, but I bowed to the Council's wisdom. I do, after all, lead only at their request."

Lady Moldar looked at him closely, eyes narrowed. *Somehow, I don't think she believes me,* Artega thought. He wondered if he had made a mistake; Lady Moldar could be a powerful enemy if she chose to become one.

But she appeared willing to let it go, this time. "Well," she said. "I suppose there was no permanent damage done."

"I understand there were no casualties," Artega said. "Let us at least be thankful for that."

"My entire household is present and accounted for, Strator," Lady Moldar replied. "Indeed, let us be thankful." She inclined her head slightly, her composure entirely intact once more. "I trust, however, that the Council will now be moved to take action."

Artega sighed heavily. "One can only hope. Rest assured, I will do my best to persuade them of the need."

"Thank you for your time, Strator Artega."

"You're most welcome, Lady Moldar."

Lady Moldar left, the door sliding closed behind her. Artega looked at it thoughtfully. "She's hiding something," he said out loud. "Something happened up there she's decided not to tell me about. Skandar?"

"Yes, Strator?"

"I'm designating Lady Moldar's household a Class C security concern. Run background scans on the personal information of all members of her household and monitor their whereabouts. Daily reports to me."

"Yes, Strator."

Artega nodded, satisfied. Such low-grade monitoring shouldn't alert Lady Moldar to his interest, and it just might turn up something interesting—possibly even a Free Forcer spy. Someone, after all, must have told the Free Forcers that the caravan was headed up the mountain road for them to intercept it so neatly.

Still no word from the Groundforce contingent trying to track the Free Forcers to their hiding place, though. "Skandar, Contact Groundforce Lieutenant Chon VYo14." Artega drummed his fingers impatiently on his desk until one of the small vidscreens lit with the young lieutenant's image. "Your report is late, Lieutenant," Artega snapped.

Lieutenant Chon looked pale. "I'm afraid we've lost the trail, Strator."

Artega stiffened. "*What?*"

"I'm sorry, Strator, but they were simply too careful."

"You must have some idea of their destination!"

"Only roughly, sir."

"Better than nothing. Comb the area! Watch for their patrols. And keep me posted!"

"Yes, sir."

Artega broke contact. "Damn! Skandar!"

"Yes, Strator."

"Double Skyforce patrols over the mountains. I want planes in the air constantly. Sooner or later, someone is bound to see something."

"Yes, Strator."

Markus, Artega thought. *Markus could find them in an hour with his battle scanners.* But Artega's needs didn't rate any consideration next to those of the Preceptorate, even though it was his planet the Preceptorate was about to reclaim.

He had a feeling it was a glimpse into his future place in the scheme of things on Avalon, and he didn't much like it.

On the other hand, if his low-tech search turned up that Rebel pilot, it should earn him more than a few points when the new/old regime took over. Politics was all about using a little bit of power to gain more. It was a game Artega played to perfection, and whoever was running Avalon, it was a game that wouldn't change. In the meantime...

"Skandar, monthly manufacturing figures, all factories," he said. "Time to get back to work."

"Yes, Strator."

———

As THE SUN set over the mountains, Tor landed his Skyforce single-seater in the silky-smooth fashion he strove to make his trademark, only the chirp as wheels touched pavement marking the transition from air to ground. "Scout A4 on the ground," he reported to the tower. "Taxiing to flight line."

"Roger, A4," responded the flight controller. "Uh, Tor, you've got a high-priority message waiting for you. Coded private. Hard-copy is waiting in your message slot in the ready room."

"Thanks, Tower." Tor frowned. It had to be Kyla. No one else would contact him. Probably still wanted to talk him out of Skyforce, wanted him to run away with her and join the Free Forcers—the same terrorists he'd just spent six hours searching for.

No chance, sister, he thought. *Not after what those bastards did to Parl. I've got a debt to pay.*

A thought occurred to him. What if she had hard information about where the Free Forcers could be found? She might have heard something from other teks.

If he could get her to tell him something like that, it would be worth putting up with her childish pleas. *She needs to grow up,* Tor thought as he guided his plane into its spot in the long flight line, and mechanics ran to meet it. *Fantasies won't cut it anymore. She has to accept the life she's been handed and make the best of it. Like I have. Maidservant to a lady is a lot better life than digging potatoes on a tekfarm. So is Skyforce.*

He climbed out of the cockpit, returned the salute of the mechanic in charge of his plane, then headed for the ready room across the blastrock of the landing field, still blackened from the starships that had landed and departed from there more than a century ago.

Inside, he stripped off his warm flying leathers, put on his blue duty uniform, poured himself a cup of stimtea from the always-hot supply, quickly perused the messages posted on the bulletin board (seeing nothing of interest), and only then went to the message slots, where eyes-only messages and orders for individual pilots were placed. He slipped his

Skyforce ID tag out from under his uniform and into the scanner alongside the slot, and a sheet of paper popped out.

He read it, then read it again. *To Skyforcer Tor XA293 from Lady Ava Moldar. Dear Tor. I'm afraid I have terrible news concerning your sister, Kyla. Please come to my townhouse at 89 Windsor Way as soon as you receive this. I'll be expecting you.*

Tor put down his stimtea and rushed out of the ready room.

As the robocab drove him to Lady Moldar's townhouse through the dark, nearly deserted streets of Skandar, Tor could only think about the last time he had seen his sister and the dreadful, silent way they had parted. What if that had been the last time he would see her, ever?

Please, God, he prayed silently, *don't let her be dead.*

But praying gave him no relief. God had never answered his prayers before.

The robocab stopped before a nondescript building at the very edge of town that looked more like a warehouse than a townhouse. Tor looked at it, then said to the robocab, "Please confirm address."

"89 Windsor Way," the cab said.

Tor frowned. "Please wait," he told the cab, and got out.

The building's outer wall was featureless brick, but there was an ordinary-looking wooden door with the number "89" on it. Tor went up to it and knocked.

It swung open silently into darkness. "Please come in, Tor," a woman's voice said.

Feeling strangely nervous, Tor did so. The moment he was inside, the door closed, and lights came up, revealing a short corridor, panelled in rich, dark wood. Another door at the far end opened. "Just a little farther, Tor," said the woman.

Tor walked to the far door, his boots making no sound on the thick white carpet, and stepped into a much larger chamber that, finally, met his expectations of what a noble lady's townhouse should look like.

Beams of dark wood overarched a room lit mainly by an enormous fireplace. More of the white, fur-like carpet covered the floor, and chairs and couches of red leather were ranged around the walls. An archway to his right led into a dining area and presumably a kitchen, while a spiral staircase in the corner climbed to a balcony, where Tor could see the tops of three other doors, all closed except one.

Directly in front of the fire, a bottle of wine and two filled glasses gleamed on a low table. From the couch behind it rose a tiny middle-aged woman, dressed in a flowing white robe that revealed disconcerting glimpses of her body as she moved.

"I'm Lady Moldar," she said. "Welcome."

"Lady Moldar," Tor said. He felt out of his element here, like a fish flopping around on the shore. "You said you had news about Kyla. Is she all right?"

"Come here. Sit with me."

Stiffly, Tor complied, sitting on the overstuffed couch and accepting the proffered glass of wine. He'd never tasted wine before—it was far too expensive for teks to drink. He sipped it cautiously, grimaced, and put the glass down. As far as he was concerned, the nobles could have it.

"Your sister," Lady Moldar said, "is missing."

Then she's not dead! Tor thought first, and then, *She did it. She ran away.* "I don't understand."

"Oh, I think you do." Lady Moldar sipped her own wine. She leaned back on the couch and pulled her legs up onto it, facing him. "Yesterday, Free Forcers attacked my caravan en route to my mountain estate. Your sister chose to join the terrorists when they fled."

She's with the terrorists who killed Parl! Tor thought. He felt sick. "Maybe she was kidnapped," he said, but he didn't really believe it.

"Please, Tor, I'm not stupid." A touch of anger heated Lady Moldar's voice. "She had obviously been in contact with the Free Forcers before. She must have been the one who told them I was coming. Of course, she ran away with them: she knew I would discover her role in the attack and have her arrested."

"Lady Moldar, I'm sure that's not—"

"Quiet!" The heat became fire. "So, I asked myself, where did she come in contact with Free Forcers? She only joined my staff a few days ago. Obviously, she came in contact with them at the tekfarm—the same tekfarm, Skyforcer, where *you* grew up."

"Milady, we heard rumours, it's true, but we never—"

"The only possible conclusion, Skyforcer," Lady Moldar said, overriding him, "is that you are a security risk. I'm quite sure my good friend, Skyforce Commander Ekar, would agree with me."

Tor went cold. They'd strip him of his wings. Lock him up. He wouldn't be able to avenge Parl.

He wouldn't be able to fly.

"But it's not true!" he whispered. "Milady, please!"

She studied him in silence for a moment, sipping her wine. Finally, she set the glass aside. "I would like to believe you, Tor," she said. "I really would. I would hate to see an innocent young man tarred with the same brush as his misguided sister. That's why I have, as yet, not reported my suspicions to anyone. I have said that my household returned intact. No one knows about your sister being with the Free Forcers—yet. Once that information is released, I'm afraid your own days in Skyforce are numbered." She moved closer to him on the couch. "How long it remains a secret depends entirely on you."

Tor looked at her. She was very close, and her robe had fallen open. "I...I don't..." *I don't understand*, he wanted to say, but it wouldn't have been true.

Lady Moldar took his hand inside her robe and cupped it around her breast. "Do we have an understanding, Skyforcer?" she said softly.

Tor closed his eyes and swallowed. *Kyla*, he thought. In different ways, the Free Forcers had taken both his best friend and his sister. Now he had no one and nothing except his flying.

Lady Moldar's skin was soft and smooth beneath his touch. She could help him or hurt him. And he'd been hurt enough.

He opened his eyes. "Yes," he said and bent to kiss the lady's lips.

10 / MOVEMENT IN THE UNDERGROWTH

MELODAN LISTENED to Kyla's story with a mixture of horror and admiration. Twice Kyla had to stop for a minute to collect herself, but she never cried. When she finished, after a moment's silence, she said, "I'm tired now. I think I'll sleep."

"Good night," Melodan replied, almost in a whisper. She watched as Kyla removed her white tunic, half-expecting to see scars on Kyla's back, despite what Kyla had said, but her skin was unmarked. Melodan shuddered. She had never heard of anything like the neural whip Kyla described, but she had heard of similar Preceptorate toys. A serf punished with such a device could continue to work, whereas a serf beaten in a more time-honoured fashion might lose productivity. And you could use the neural whip as often as you liked without the risk of permanent injury.

Kyla will help me stop the Preceptorate from reclaiming this planet, Melodan thought, watching her roommate's even breathing; not surprisingly, Kyla had fallen asleep almost the instant she lay down. *And Kyla has a brother. A twin named Tor—in Skyforce. Inside the spaceport fence.*

Right where I have to go.

She undressed and got into bed, resolving to talk to Rand in the morning. She had waited long enough.

But Rand obviously didn't think so. When she and Kyla, after scrounging breakfast, went to the colonel, they found him sitting on a stump outside his hut, examining a circuit board Melodan guessed was part of the loot from the caravan. He looked up as they approached. "Sleep well?"

"Yes, sir," said Kyla. Melodan merely nodded.

"Good. Vik!" The boy came around the corner. He looked even more pale and sullen than usual. "Take Kyla out into the fields and start teaching her how to use a rifle. And start her on self-defence, too." Vik jerked a quick nod, then led her off without a word.

Melodan remained where she was, and Rand raised one eyebrow. "Something I can do for you?"

"Rand, this can't go on," she said. "We're wasting time. There's a Preceptorate cruiser in this system, remember? If I don't warn the rebels, you could have the Preceptor himself here—and that would mean the end of your little guerilla experiment. A single reconnaissance satellite could find you, and one Swordcraft could turn this whole valley into slag. You can't fight the Preceptorate with plastic rifles and knives!"

Rand's eyes narrowed, and Melodan suddenly knew she had made a mistake. "We've fought the Preceptorate for fifteen years," he growled. "And we'll keep on fighting—with sticks and stones if we have to. You're asking me to throw away the lives of people who trust me, and I won't do it." He pointed to the fields. "Right now, nothing is as important as harvest. Without it, we starve this winter. If you want to earn our help, I suggest you start swinging a scythe!"

Melodan persisted. "But, Colonel, listen! Kyla's brother is in Skyforce—at the spaceport. He could get me inside—"

"Even Kyla doesn't trust Kyla's brother!" Rand snapped. "I won't hear any more. Get to work or get out of my sight!"

Melodan opened her mouth to argue some more, then closed it with a snap and turned away, vowing silently that the battle wasn't over.

In the hope of proving herself an ally, she reported to work in the fields, though she knew nothing about scything or what the Free Forcers called "stooking," gathering the cut grain into tall upright bundles more easily loaded on wagons for the trip to the threshing floor. But having grown up on a ranch, she was no stranger to hard work, and soon she was swinging the sharp curved blade with the best of them, though she wished the Free Forcers had at least managed to acquire a horse-drawn swather, if not a tractor.

Why not a fully automated field robot while you're at it? she asked herself wryly. *How would you get large machinery into this valley without heavy-lift aircraft?* The answer, of course, was that she wouldn't—it was impossible. She quit dreaming about it and kept swinging.

Over the next few days, she settled into a routine. While Kyla and Vik went off together to train, Melodan and just about every other able-bodied person over the age of twelve reported to the fields to scythe wheat or pick corn. And gradually, it seemed to Melodan that the adult Free Forcers were indeed warming to her a little.

The children warmed more quickly. Although to begin

with, they watched her shyly from a distance, giggling, on the second day, some of the boldest began asking her questions, and it wasn't long before she was regaling them with tales of the galaxy. A few mothers took their children away at first, but those same youngsters soon returned —with their parents, who somehow contrived to stay in earshot as she retold tales of her father's great battles. Only Rand kept completely remote, frowning as he watched her but not putting a stop to her storytelling.

Yet, despite her resolve to prove her trustworthiness, her restlessness grew day by day. Time was wasting, and nothing was being done. Who knew how soon the Preceptorate would be ready to move? Certainly, sooner than the RSF would come looking for her in a "safe" sector. In a few months, if she didn't report, a follow-up mission *might* be sent—or her loss might be marked down to an accident. *Pilot error*, she thought bitterly. *Incompetence.*

And the worst of it was, it would be the truth.

Her father would never forgive her.

KYLA KNEW Melodan was frustrated and unhappy—the pilot didn't exactly keep her feelings secret in their hut at night—but for her, the first few days after she joined the Free Forcers were the happiest of her life.

Vik proved to be an excellent teacher, remarkably patient with her initial ineptitude. To his surprise, and certainly to her own, she learned hand-to-hand combat quickly. She discovered she had an excellent sense of balance and a good memory for the moves he showed her.

To be sure, she never rose above mediocrity when it came to shooting, but at least she didn't drop the rifle again after the first round she fired, when the noise and recoil, even though Vik had warned her about it, frightened her half to death.

She found Vik intriguing. Most of the time, he was as silent and withdrawn as he had been when she first met him after the attack on Lady Moldar's caravan. But occasionally —a couple of times when she unexpectedly succeeded in taking him down and once when a flock of silverwings swung overhead, glittering in the morning sun—she caught glimpses of something else underneath, of a very different young man, one with a crooked grin that lit up his face and eyes that could sparkle with delight and wonder.

But they were only glimpses; almost immediately, they vanished beneath the taciturn gloom he seemed to wrap around himself like a shroud.

She found him fascinating and wished sometimes, as he leaned over her after having thrown her to the ground, that there might be something in his eyes other than a professional interest in her skill or lack of it. The more time she spent with him, the more she would have liked some indication that he was aware of her as a girl and not just a student— but he never showed any interest.

Melodan commiserated with her but couldn't suggest any solution. "He's messed up pretty bad, I think," she said one night in the hut. "His mother's dead, and I think he blames his father—but his father is also his commanding officer. He needs time to work through all that before he's going to notice you or any other girl."

Kyla sat on her bed, stripping and cleaning the rifle she'd

been issued. "I'm probably just being silly. He's the first boy close to my own age I've ever known except Tor, so of course, I'm attracted to him—but I don't even know if I *like* him. There's nothing there to like, not on the surface, just this perfect little Free Forcer...only I think there's something more there underneath, and that's what looks interesting. If I could just get under his skin..."

Melodan laughed. "One thing at a time. First, get hold of his skin, then maybe what's underneath will follow."

Kyla blushed and threw the cleaning rag at her.

After two weeks, Rand judged Kyla's training advanced enough to send her on a scouting patrol with Vik and Tara. As they walked along the river, they passed Melodan, stooking in one of the scythed fields. Kyla waved, and Melodan waved back, straightening for a moment to watch them.

"Get back to work!" Tara shouted. Melodan folded her arms and glared. Kyla grinned at her from behind Tara's back; even Vik half-smiled.

They headed west, climbing up a narrow trail that switchbacked alongside the waterfall, then following the gorge through which the river flowed, and finally climbing out of it up onto a ridge where someone had reported seeing smoke the day before. Tara led the way without ever looking back, and Kyla fell farther and farther behind. Her training with Vik had toughened her up considerably, but she still wasn't used to long hikes, especially not carrying a rifle, which seemed to snag every outthrust branch. And how come the vines at ground level only wrapped themselves around *her* ankles and not around Tara's or Vik's?

She glared after Tara, but there was no way she would

ask the sharp-tongued woman to slow down for her. Nor would she ask Vik. He'd just stare at her silently and shrug. She struggled on and eventually lost sight of her companions altogether.

Finally, she stopped in a small clearing, panting. She knew she could find her way back to the village without any trouble, but that was hardly the point. She was supposed to be an integral part of this scouting party, damn it. She started to shout but thought better of it at the last minute and closed her mouth. She could just imagine what Tara and Vik would say about *that*.

Better to stay put. Sooner or later, they'd notice she wasn't with them anymore and come back for her.

She sat down on a handy rock and pulled out her canteen. As she raised it to her lips, she heard a twig snap, and a bird rose, whirring, out of the forest to her left.

There they are, she thought, and hastily took a swallow from the canteen and put it away.

A second later, Tara and Vik appeared—from the forest to her *right*.

Kyla stared at them, then snatched up her rifle and started toward the place where she'd heard the first sound. Tara charged across the clearing behind her, grabbed her arm, and spun her around. "You stupid tek," Tara snarled. "Why didn't you keep up?"

Kyla felt her face flush. "Why didn't you notice I hadn't, patrol *leader*?" she snapped. "Isn't that your job—*ma'am*?"

"Listen, you—" Tara started, but Vik interrupted.

"She's right, Tara," he said. "As patrol leader, you should have known she was having problems. It's her first patrol. Lighten up."

It was Tara's turn to flush. "Listen, *boy*, I may have to take orders from your father, but I don't have to take them from you!"

Vik's eyes narrowed; then, he spun and stalked off. Tara glared after him, then turned to Kyla and said, "Let's move out. And this time, I'm bringing up the rear to make sure you keep up!"

"There's something I have to check out first, *ma'am*," Kyla said and set off to where she'd heard the noise in the bushes again.

Furiously, Tara stalked after her. "What do you think you're doing?" she yelled.

Kyla didn't look back. "I heard something in the forest. Just before you came shouting into the clearing."

"An animal," Tara said dismissively.

"Maybe." The birds had flown up from a distinctive orange tree. She went to the tree and stared at the ground, but it just looked like ground to her. She didn't even know what she was looking for. She sniffed the air, but all she could smell was the rather overpowering bacon-like odour of the tree's fiery leaves.

Vik suddenly came striding back across the clearing. Tara explained what was going on and ordered him to check for spoor. He shoved Kyla aside, looked around for less than a minute, and growled, "An animal."

"You heard him," Tara said when Kyla would have searched more. "He's one of the best trackers we've got. It was an animal. Now let's get moving. We're still five kilometres from where they saw that smoke."

"You'd both better be right," Kyla muttered as they left the clearing behind them.

Lieutenant Chon's face appeared on Strator Artega's bedside vidscreen. For once it wasn't pale, even in the flaring light of a military tent-torch. "Good news, Strator!" he announced, beaming. "We have them! A scout stumbled on one of their patrols and tracked it back to an unmapped village in a valley not far from here. Your orders, Strator?"

At last, Artega thought. *At last!* "How long will it take your troops to get there?"

"Two days, Strator."

"Too long. There's always the possibility they spotted your man." Artega frowned, thinking. "I'll order a Skyforce strike for tomorrow morning. Move in and mop up as soon as possible."

"Yes, Strator!"

"Skandar?"

"I heard, Strator," said the AI. "Time of attack?"

"Mid-morning. I want to make sure they're up and about." He smiled. "I want to them to know what hit them."

"Yes, Strator."

"Good night, Skandar."

"Good night, Strator."

Artega yawned and went back to a sleep suddenly full of pleasant dreams.

MORNING CAME FAR TOO EARLY for Tor, in his own bunk barely three hours after yet another night in Lady Moldar's townhouse. *The woman is insatiable*, he thought, rolling over in bed with a groan, the clang of the wake-up bell ringing counterpoint to the throbbing in his head. And he thought he'd pulled a muscle in his lower back...

Patrol Leader Levof pounded on the side of his bunk. "Rise and shine, Skyforcer," he said. "No more searching for terrorists today. Groundforce found 'em."

That brought Tor wide awake and upright, despite the stab of pain in his back. "What?"

"Orders from Skandar. We're to take 'em out. And I'd like you to fly my right wing." Levoff grinned. "We've both got a score to settle, don't we?"

"Parl," Tor said. "Thank you, sir!"

"Get a move on. Breakfast in five minutes and mission briefing in thirty. We take off at 0930."

It wasn't until Tor was already in his flight leathers and jogging to the mess hall that it occurred to him to wonder where Kyla was. The thought that she might be on the receiving end of his guns today stabbed his heart with a pain every bit as sharp as the one in his lower back.

Her choice, he thought grimly. *She has to live with the consequences.*

As did he.

———

MELODAN SWUNG HER SCYTHE FURIOUSLY, felling a big swath of wheat but also earning an angry glance from Tara, working to her left. Melodan ignored her.

Three weeks! she thought bitterly. Three weeks on Avalon, with the Preceptorate setting its claws deeper and deeper into the system, and all she had done was farm. Everyone except Tara seemed to have accepted her, but still, Rand refused to help her and had her watched so closely there was no hope of sneaking out of the valley and trying on her own.

It was intolerable, especially now when she had a possible way to get into the spaceport. She paused and glanced through a windbreak of trees into the next field, where Kyla worked. She had said nothing to Kyla of her thoughts—the younger girl preferred not to talk about her brother. But she was sure once she knew how important it was...

But before she could approach Kyla, she had to convince Rand, and Rand wouldn't listen. She took another violent swipe at the golden wheat. She was a pilot, not a farmhand!

"That does it!" Tara threw down her scythe and faced her. "You almost took my leg off!"

Melodan's rage suddenly had a focus. She dropped her own blade before she could be tempted to swing it at the Free Forcer. "So keep your distance!"

"I'm going to—" Tara began, then stopped suddenly, staring over Melodan's shoulder.

"Come on!" Melodan said fiercely. She'd show this—

But Tara screamed, "Skyforce!"

"What?" Melodan spun, and saw them—a dozen biplanes, streaming over the cleft in the valley wall that marked the gorge.

Free Forcers all through the fields dropped their tools and dashed for cover. Tara snatched her rifle from her shoulder and ran for the windbreak, Melodan right behind her.

Kyla plunged in among the trees with them as the first aircraft roared over, guns chattering. Dirt fountained in twin lines through the wheat and trees, and someone screamed. As Tara fired uselessly after the plane, twisting to follow it, Melodan watched it bank sharply right, over the huts. Fire and smoke blossomed beneath it, and a dull boom shook the air a moment later.

Tara swore, scrambled up, and ran toward the village.

"Tara! Get down!" Melodan cried, but the thunder of engines drowned her voice as six more planes swept toward them, wingtip to wingtip, firing as they came. She clung to the shaking ground, dirt and dead leaves showering her head. When she looked up, her gaze met Kyla's wide eyes over the twisted root of a bush.

The planes made run after run over the clustered huts. As Melodan watched, the walls of the house she shared with Kyla exploded outward in smoking shards. Others followed, and more and more Free Forcers burst from the windbreak and ran toward the village, in an instinctive, futile attempt to defend their homes. For about two seconds Melodan watched, thinking how foolish they were—then Kyla suddenly leaped up and dashed away, too, and an instant later she followed. Futile though it was, she couldn't hide in the trees while the others fought.

From somewhere in the burning village a missile streaked skyward, and a diving Skyforce plane exploded into a thousand flaming pieces that plunged into a cornfield. Melodan heard herself cheering at the top of her voice.

She was brought to a startled halt a moment later by a moan. Her eyes followed a trail of broken stalks into the wheat, and she plunged into the field—then fell headlong over something in the furrows. Spitting dirt, she rolled over...and suddenly, she couldn't breathe.

Tara lay there like a shattered china doll, her clothes and the wheat and even the black earth beneath her soaked with blood. With a moan of her own, Melodan scrambled toward Tara on hands and knees and carefully rolled her over. Her hands came away red and sticky.

Tara's ragged breath bubbled in her throat and in a huge sucking hole in her chest. Her eyelids flicked open but her eyes tracked aimlessly. She whispered something, and Melodan bent close.

"Tell...Marik...love him," she heard, then Tara suddenly stiffened, her fingers clutching the blood-soaked earth spasmodically. An instant later she fell limp and her rasping breath ceased.

Explosions racked the valley and the crackle of rifle fire echoed from the cliffs, but Melodan felt enveloped in dreadful silence as she knelt alone with Tara's lifeless body...until one of the planes swung low over the field. She looked up as it approached, wondering vaguely why metal tanks were slung beneath its wings—then screamed as a sheet of fire exploded through the wheat and roared toward her like a hungry animal. Shocked out of her stupor, she scrambled up and tried to drag Tara's body into the open, but she was too weak and the fire too close. At the last possible moment, she gave up and ran out of the field, coughing on acrid smoke. Almost on her heels, the fire swept through the place where she had been.

Rage suddenly filled her, and she tore the pocket on her thigh ripping the blazer from the place she'd kept it hidden all these weeks.

Her thumb on the security lock snapped open the lid, and she snatched out the silvery weapon that nestled in the black foam inside. A thin black cord connected it to its power supply, a grey box she clipped to a belt loop. A green digital readout on the box showed it had full power. Gripping the weapon so tightly her hand hurt, Melodan ran toward the battle.

Every field was burning now; the fire which had chased her from Tara's side pursued her into the village. She pressed her back tight against a shattered wall. The bombs had stopped falling, but still the planes circled like carrion-birds, shooting at anything that moved.

Despite the destruction, she saw only one or two bodies in the ruins. *Almost everyone was in the fields*, she thought. *Everyone except—*

"No," she whispered, then screamed, "No!" and ran toward the north end of the village—

—toward the school.

Rand was crossing the village green when the Skyforce planes screamed into the valley. In that first instant, he felt not so much shock as a strange relief.

It was over. The years of hiding were over.

In the next instant, terror filled him as he realized what the attack would mean. "Skyforce!" he screamed, with a dozen other voices. Most of the Free Forcers were in the fields, but the elderly couple he'd seen by the fire the night he'd returned from the attack on Lady Moldar's caravan were in the green with him; he ran to them and hurried them into the trees, away from the buildings that would surely be the primary targets.

He was right about that. As the biplanes thundered over, the first bomb ripped through the roof of his house. An instant later the roof lifted with a roar, the walls blew outward in a cascade of broken brick, and the front door sailed across the green, snapping in two as it slammed against the corner of another house.

As flames licked at the splintered beams he had raised so many years ago, more bombs claimed other buildings in the village. Leaving the old couple clinging to each other at the base of a tree, he ran to the edge of the grove, where he could see the fields.

Planes banked at the end of the valley and raced back, tracers lashing through the wheat. A woman running toward him screamed and went down, her scythe arcing through the air as she fell. He started toward her, but another plane came over, with silver tanks slung beneath its wings, and liquid fire suddenly sheeted across the field. Even above the roar of the flames he heard the wounded woman scream again, a scream that died away in choking agony.

Helplessly, he clung to the tree beside him as the planes made pass after pass. No one moved, now, in the fields; the Free Forcers who were still alive had taken whatever shelter they could find. Skyforcer planes carried limited bomb loads—part of the Battlefield Agreements that limited the level of technology available to the military—so the first pass had exhausted their explosives. Now the strafing died away, as well, but the plane with the silver tanks, having scorched every field, apparently hadn't exhausted its load. It banked over the gorge, then flew back toward the village, some final target having caught the pilot's eye.

But what? Rand made his way back to the green. Thatched roofs blazed. It made no difference whether the buildings had been hit directly or not, the flames would claim them. There was nothing left to set afire, nothing but...

...but one building, set a little apart from the others, and at the extreme west end of the village. By the time the flight had reached it, their bombs had been dropped, so it still stood intact, an inviting target...

...and even from here he could see the frightened faces of children looking out its windows.

Fresh terror choked him. "Get them out! Get them out!" he screamed, running toward the school, but he could hear the napalm-carrying plane roaring up behind him, overtaking him, there was no way those children would get out of—

—and then, suddenly, Melodan was in front of him, between him and the school, holding something that glittered silver even in the smoke-dimmed sunlight. "Get down!" she screamed, and as he flung himself to the ground the object in her hand flashed blue-green fire as bright as lightning.

He rolled over in time to see the napalm plane explode in mid-air into a huge ball of black-and-orange flame. Flaming debris rained down on the village, a chunk of blackened ceramic from the engine thudded into the ground just a metre from his foot—but then the attack was over, and the children were safe.

The other Skyforce planes banked away and fled back the way they had come, quickly disappearing behind the wall of smoke rising above the valley.

Rand stood up, feeling like an old, old man, coughing in the smoke. Melodan stood shaking and blowing on her hands; her weapon lay on the ground, smoking, obviously overloaded and useless. Behind her, children had spilled out of the schoolhouse and were staring at her, but their teachers kept them back.

Rand went to her. "Thank you," he said.

"I couldn't let anything happen to the children," she said, sounding dazed. "I couldn't...they accepted me."

"And I didn't. I know." Rand looked at the destruction all around. "This is all my fault," he said bitterly. "I knew this could happen—almost certainly *would* happen—someday. I should never have let my Forcers bring their families up here. We should have stayed a pure guerilla army. We wanted to have the fruits of victory without actually winning the war. But the war...the war has caught up with us."

"War has a way of doing that," Melodan said. "When you least expect it. Look what happened to me." She flexed her burned fingers and winced. "What now?"

Rand looked around. Free Forcers were starting to

emerge from hiding, searching out the wounded. For now, that was all they could think about. But soon—every soon—they had to know what he planned next.

"Groundforce must be on its way," he said, thinking out loud. "Artega knows the limitations of air power. We have to be out of the valley before tomorrow morning. He'll be counting on us having no place to go."

"Do you?"

"Yes." Rand looked up at the mountain peaks west of the valley. "We'll go back to the place we should never have left—back to the caves where we first hid when we deserted the Battlefield. Cramped, uncomfortable—but secure, even from detection from orbit."

"How far...?"

"Not far." But maybe too far, with children, old people and the wounded. How many more would they lose before they got there? How many more would die because of decisions he had made fifteen years ago? As Lissa had died. "In any event, you're not coming with us."

"I'm not?" Melodan stood very still. "Where am I going?"

"Where I should have helped you get in the first place." Rand looked east, the direction Skyforce had taken. "To the spaceport."

Kyla found Vik sitting on a rock in what had been the village green, staring at the ruins of his house.

A bandage showing a single bright-red spot of blood

bound his head but that injury couldn't possibly be severe enough to cause the kind of pain she glimpsed on his face.

She limped over to him—she'd twisted her ankle slightly in a furrow when she'd jumped up from Melodan and run toward the village—and sat down beside him.

She wanted to comfort him, but she had nothing to say. Instead, hesitantly, she reached out and took his right hand, expecting him to snatch it away...but he didn't.

Instead, his fingers tightened convulsively on hers, as though he desperately needed something, anything, to hold on to.

Linked, they sat in silence and watched his house burn.

MARBLE ECHOED to Strator Artega's footsteps as he strode into the Chamber of the Noble Council and approached the long oval table of smoked glass. The twelve councillors seated around it had, he knew, been waiting for him for twenty minutes. Their mingled perfumes and colognes choked the air with floral scent.

Even his supporters frowned at him as he took his place at the table's foot. "I am sorry for the delay, noble councillors, but I have important news."

"You had better," muttered Lord Pelgar, a balding, portly man of advanced age and one of those who owed Lady Moldar money.

"The noble councillors must judge that for themselves," said Artega. "May I dispense with formal procedure and move at once to the matter in question?" He paused, and, when no one disagreed, said, "Skandar, activate vidscreen."

"Yes, Strator." The deep voice reverberated from the stone walls of the chamber, once the ballroom of an expensive hotel, and an abstract tapestry of grey and gold to Artega's right swept aside from an enormous vidscreen, glowing softly blue.

"Noble councillors, this was recorded earlier today. Strator, display vidrecord SF-094A."

"Yes, Strator."

As the screen lit with images of the destruction of the Free Forcer village, Artega leaned back in his chair, savouring the sense that he had reasserted his control. Groundforce would enter the valley in the morning. The Free Forcers were finished.

The vidrecord ended before the blazer beam destroyed a fireplane. Artega had no intention of showing the Council *that*. He stood as the tapestry swept back into place. "Noble councillors, the terrorist threat has been eliminated," he said. "Groundforce will arrive for mopping up by mid-day tomorrow."

"You should have delayed the Skyforce attack until Groundforce was in position for immediate follow-up," said Lord Pelgar. "What if the terrorists simply hide higher in the mountains?"

"Had I delayed, I would have lost the element of surprise," Artega said. "No force large enough to take that valley could have been moved within a day's journey without being detected. As for your other concern—if the terrorists flee into the mountains, they will starve. We have destroyed their crops, and winter is coming. I assure you, Honourable Councillors, the Free Forcer threat has been eliminated." Lady Esta, one of his staunchest supporters—thanks in part to the recent appointment of several of her relatives to minor government positions—started applauding.

After a moment, the rest of the Councillors joined in, Pelgar last, his clapping noticeably perfunctory.

Artega let the applause last just long enough, then motioned for silence with both hands. "You're too kind, my lords and ladies," he said. "And possibly premature."

"What? But you said—" Pelgar began to bluster.

"The *external* threat has been abolished," Artega said. "But let us not forget they had help from within the city; they must have, to have known when and where to strike at Lady Moldar. Noble councillors, there are traitors among our citizens."

Lady Mysta, a plump women in late middle age who was attempting to hide both conditions, cleared her throat. "A serious allegation, Strator. Have you any evidence?"

"Certainly," said Artega. "We know it was a tek named Kyla who told the Free Forcers of Lady Moldar's trip into the mountains, because she rejoined the terrorists after the attack. This fact Lady Moldar deliberately withheld from her official reports on the attack. I only discovered it when Skandar informed me that Lady Moldar had requested a new maid just two days after the attack—less than a week after she had last requested one. Further surveillance revealed that Kyla had disappeared, and discrete questioning of other members of the household staff told us when and where.

"Discovering this, I had Skandar delve further into Lady Moldar's original acquisition of Kyla. I discovered that when Lady Moldar first requested a maid, just days before Kyla's lifetask was due to be assigned, she specified age and physical appearance so narrowly that this Kyla was the only tek suitable. It might have been coincidence—but with all other considerations taken into account, I find that impossible to believe." Artega paused for effect. "Noble councillors, Lady Moldar deliberately smuggled a traitor into the city!"

"Preposterous!" exploded Pelgar. "Utterly preposterous! They raided *her* caravan!"

"What better way for a terrorist sympathizer to deliver supplies?" Artega asked. "Obviously Lady Moldar carried more than household goods on that trip. I can only guess what her real cargo was—guns, perhaps, or medicine, or electronics. But she dared not contact the Free Force directly to arrange the delivery; far too dangerous. She needed someone who could go into the city unremarked and pass a message to a terrorist spy, who in turn could pass it on to the Free Forcers. Who better than a tek—who is really a terrorist herself?"

"But the girl could not have been here more than two or three days," Lady Mysta objected.

"On her very first day Lady Moldar provided her with a wheeler and sent her—alone!—into the city."

"On what pretext?" asked Lady Elda.

"To see her brother in Skyforce."

"What?" exploded Pelgar. "Now you're telling us this supposed terrorist has a brother in *Skyforce*?"

"Indeed. And she did, in fact, see him; but she had time to see others, too. Which, obviously, she did."

Silence gripped the chamber. Even Lady Moldar's supporters had nothing to say. But Artega waited for the inevitable question, and Lady Esta did not disappoint him.

She coughed first. "What do we do with her, then?"

Artega let the silence hang for a moment, then said diffidently, "If I may make a suggestion..."

"Please," said Pelgar irritably.

"Do nothing. Whatever she thought to gain, she lost today with the destruction of the Free Forcers. But let her know that we suspect her and will watch her closely. If we do, I think we will have no more trouble from her." *Certainly I won't, at least. And if I do...* He smiled. Skandar's surveillance had also netted him information about exactly what Lady Moldar did in her Skandar City townhouse—and with whom.

Lady Elda nodded slowly. "An excellent and humane suggestion. Any discussion?" Silence. "All in favour?" Hand by reluctant hand went up.

"What about this tek's brother in Skyforce?" asked Pelgar querulously. "He could be dangerous..."

"I think I can put your fears to rest, Councillor," Artega replied. He pointed to the covered vidscreen. "That recording was made from his plane."

TOR WOKE PANIC-STRICKEN, sweating, heart pounding, and stared for a long moment in blank terror at the stars above his head, unable to remember where he was.

But then Lady Moldar stirred by his side in the wide, simsilk-sheeted bed, and everything fell into place. He was in Lady Moldar's townhouse, and the stars overhead were artificial, pinpricks of light in the black ceiling of her bedroom.

He glanced at her in the dim illumination. She lay with his back to him, curled in a fetal position; she didn't stir as he got out of bed.

Naked, he padded into the bathroom, closed the door,

turned on the light, and splashed cold water on his face. His heart rate was slowly returning to normal, and the cold sweat on his skin was drying, but his eyes looked haunted, and his face...

He hardly recognized himself. He looked...haggard. Old. Far older than his years; far older than he had any right to look.

He clicked off the light and returned to the bedroom but didn't go back to bed. Instead, he sat in a chair and looked at the sleeping form of Lady Moldar.

She'd been fiercely pleased at the success of their raid on the Free Forcer camp today. So had he. Their lovemaking had been...violent. Exhausting.

But in his dreams, the images had come back to him, the people running and dying in the fields beneath his guns, the village on fire, flames roaring through the wheat, devouring the green trees.

In his dreams, he had seen the one thing he had most dreaded to see during the attack, the one possibility he had tried to blot out of his mind: he had seen Kyla die beneath his guns.

If she had been down there, he had never spotted her during the attack, but that meant nothing. She could be dead —he might even have killed her—and he would never know.

And Parl was still dead, and now, so was Rafe, who had flown the fireplane.

All this death and destruction, just so Lady Moldar could sleep soundly in luxury.

In the darkness of the bedroom, Tor glared at her, the only person he hated more than himself.

13 / A NEW HOPE

Two hours after the attack, Melodan gathered in the village green with the other survivors for Rand's council of war.

By that time, they had counted the grim toll exacted by the Skyforcers. Tara's message of love to Mark went undelivered; he was dead, too. So were ten others—five men, three women, and two children, who had been kept home ill from school and died in their burning hut with their mother.

A grey, sour-smelling veil of smoke hung over the valley as the diminished and dispirited Free Forcers huddled together, surrounded by the smouldering ruins of their homes. Melodan's scorched hands still throbbed slightly, but no blisters had formed. She'd gotten off lightly. Almost everyone else she could see bore some more obvious mark from the attack; burns, bruises, or bandages. A few severely injured men and women lay on the ground a few metres away, their occasional moans punctuating the silence of the others, who stared blankly at Rand, seemingly sapped of strength and emotion alike. Even the children were quiet, clinging to their surviving parents.

Rand rose, face bleak. "Our situation is critical," he said baldly. "Our crop is lost. Winter is coming on. Skyforce could return at any time...and Groundforce must be on the way." He paused, looking from face to face. "We must leave this valley tonight."

"But the children," a woman said. "And the wounded..."

Rand turned toward her. "Will you throw yourself on the Strator's mercy?" he snarled so savagely that Melodan was taken aback. He spread his arms, taking in the destruction around them. "*This* is the Strator's mercy!"

The Free Forcers looked at one another uncomfortably.

Rand glared at them. "When we first fled the Battlefield, we learned the art of hiding. Skyforce and Groundforce both pursued us—and we evaded them. We can do so again." He pointed north. "We can hide in the caves where we hid fifteen years ago. There's water and game. We can survive!"

"Not through the winter!" a man protested. "A few weeks, maybe—"

"A few weeks will be enough." Rand glanced at Melodan, back at the others. "Our hand has been forced. We can no longer bide our time, hoping our few contacts in the city and among the tekfarms can build our support to the point where we can lead a revolution. Perhaps that was a fool's dream.

"Instead, we have a new hope—desperate, but one that could free us forever." He turned and nodded, and Melodan, her heart suddenly pounding, stood up.

"You have allies among the stars," she began. "They have

suffered as you have today. They will help you—if we can contact them.

"Eventually, someone will come looking for me, but it could be weeks or months. We can't wait. Not only because of what happened today, but because the Preceptorate is already here and will soon be here in force—and what you have suffered under the rule of the Strator is only the beginning of the suffering the Preceptorate will bring.

"To prevent that, I must warn the Revolutionary Space Force. That means I have to get into the spaceport control tower. It will have an emergency dimspace transmitter. Using it, I can warn my people, and within days they can be here with a force that will make all the planes of all the Cities on Avalon look like a swarm of—of skreekers." She paused. "But to get into the spaceport tower, we'll have to infiltrate Skybase."

Muttering ran through the crowd. "How?" shouted someone. "Knock on the gate?" There was bitter laughter.

"Something like that." Melodan looked at Kyla. "A Skyforce pilot is going to let me in."

KYLA STARED BACK AT MELODAN, for a moment not understanding what she meant; then it hit her.

Melodan thought Tor would help them get into Skybase.

It won't work, she thought sickly. *Doesn't she understand? Tor believes in Skyforce. He's forgotten all about being a tek.*

But he's still your brother, another part of her argued. *He can't have changed that much. He won't turn you over to the Forcers; he couldn't.*

That doesn't mean he'll help.

But he might.

He might. Was that enough on which to hang all the hopes of the Free Forcers?

She looked around at the bitter faces of the people she had come to think of as friends and comrades over the last three weeks; lastly, at Vik, sitting beside her, his expression as bleak and barren as the scorched fields behind them.

A desperate hope was better than no hope at all, and without Melodan's plan, no hope existed.

She met Melodan's gaze. "Tell me what you want me to do."

AS NIGHT FELL, the Free Forcers fled, bearing their wounded in litters or on horseback. Only three would make the journey to the spaceport: Melodan, Kyla, and Vik, whom Rand took aside before the trio separated from the main force.

With the grim caravan waiting in the background, dark shadows in the fading light, Rand faced his son...and discovered he didn't know what to say. Vik hadn't spoken to him since the Skyforce attack; had hardly spoken to him since that night by the fire three weeks ago.

"I...know you didn't mean it when you said you hated me," Rand said finally. He hoped he was right. "You're confused about how you should feel about me right now because you blame me for so many things...but son, know this: I love you. Be careful. Don't let anything happen to you. If I lost you, too..." His voice choked off. He swallowed hard, then said, "Good luck, son," and held out his hand.

Vik looked at it, looked at him—then turned and walked away.

Rand watched him rejoin Melodan and Kyla, then turned back to the main force, feeling as if he'd been stabbed in the heart.

It was just another drop in his vast inner reservoir of pain. Sometimes he wondered how long it would be before the dam broke and the pain overwhelmed him.

MELODAN, watching Vik turn his back on his father's outstretched hand, thought of her own father and felt a sharp, unexpected pang of sadness. Biting her lip, she glanced at Kyla, who stared at the ground.

"Tell me what you want me to do," the other girl had said. Unfortunately, Melodan couldn't—not specifically. All she knew was that Kyla had to convince her brother to help them get into the spaceport—and preferably out again. "Can you really get through to him?" she asked Kyla in confidence after the council of war.

"He's my brother," Kyla had replied. "He'll listen."

But will he help? Melodan wondered now, looking at her. Just because someone was family didn't mean they'd help you or even understand you. Look at Vik and Rand.

Look at her and her father.

Vik rejoined them. "Let's go," he snarled and led the way into the woods.

Full darkness soon descended, but the stars blazed in a clear sky, providing enough light for them to follow the game trail Vik had found. "We'll travel due east," Vik had told them before they set out. "Once we're clear of the mountains, we'll approach the city through the tekfarms. If we stay to the buffer woods, no one should see us, and any that do will take us for Groundforcers and mind their own business."

After an hour or so of slow but steady travel through the black wood, Vik called a halt. "We'll camp here," he said. "No fire."

They sat in a tight little circle to eat their cold rations of bread and meat, then Kyla and Melodan lay down close to each other while Vik took the first watch. Melodan fell asleep almost at once, waking to Vik shaking her arm. "Your watch," he said and lay down in the depression her body had left in the thick grass.

Two hours later, she woke Kyla, and grabbed more fitful sleep before coming awake in the pre-dawn light from a nightmare (in which Skyforce figured prominently) to the chilling realization that the sound she heard was real, not left-over dream-stuff.

"Into the woods!" Vik cried, coming awake beside her, and all three of them scrambled under cover as the planes roared directly overhead.

"Are they looking for us?" Kyla asked breathlessly.

"They're going back to the valley!" Vik stood, watching them speed toward the east. "Probably to support a Groundforce assault."

"Only they'll find nothing to assault," Melodan said with grim satisfaction. "The Free Forcers are gone."

"But they were travelling at night with wounded and children," Vik said. "They won't be far gone. I hope—"

Melodan touched his shoulder. "There's nothing you can do."

He stiffened. "I know that," he snapped. "Let's march."

Almost slipped, didn't you? Melodan thought, watching him as they set out west again. *Almost showed emotion, like a real human being.*

She watched Kyla move up beside him and talk to him in a low voice, once touching him on the shoulder just as Melodan had, but from *her* touch, he didn't flinch. *Good for you,* Melodan thought. *That boy needs someone to slip inside his armour. If he stays as hard and brittle as he is now, one of these days, he's going to shatter—and I don't want it to be when I'm depending on him.*

In that thought, she heard the echo of her father talking about men in his squadron, and she frowned.

Half an hour later, the planes streamed past in the other direction, and Melodan, hiding with the others, glanced west, wondering if their mission to save the Free Forcers had already failed.

By sundown, they were in low hills and emerged from the forest onto open land. To their right rose a fence of plastic mesh. Lights twinkled from low buildings across a stubbled field, and the smell of woodsmoke drifted to them. Melodan sniffed it and felt suddenly homesick for warm evenings around the ranch-house fireplace with the winter wind raging helplessly outside, and those rare nights on the trail with her father when the Revolution had seemed locked safely away among the distant, twinkling stars. Only at those times had she felt truly close to him, and there had never been enough of them—not enough to make up for all those other nights when she had heard her mother crying, alone, through the dark hours.

Her own thoughts startled her. *It was war!* she told herself fiercely. *He did what he had to. Just like I am.*

"We'll camp here," said Vik.

Kyla watched Vik as they ate their cold, comfortless supper. In their own camp, they had to be content with only the smell of woodsmoke. He was so tense, so unhappy —too unhappy, even for their dire circumstances. She'd thought she was getting through to him yesterday when they had sat together holding hands, but since then, he'd been as cold and withdrawn as ever. It was all tied up with his father and with his mother's death, but she hadn't figured it all out yet. She thought if she could just understand why Vik felt the way he did, she might be able to break away a little of his shell and get at the soft heart hidden inside.

When he finished eating, he wandered off a little way and sat with his back to a tree. Kyla got up and walked over to him. A twig snapped under her foot, and Vik started, then saw her and relaxed.

"May I join you?" she asked.

"If you want to."

Kyla sat beside him for a few minutes in silence broken only by the wind rustling the dead stalks in the field beyond the fence. "Can I ask you something?" she said at last.

Vik grunted.

"How did your father meet your mother? A Ground-forcer and a noble's servant...it's an odd combination."

Vik sat silent for a moment, and she thought he was going to get up and walk away, but finally, he said, "They met at one of those huge patriotic rallies the Strator stages before the start of every Battlefield season. My father had already acquired a reputation as a promising young officer, so he was formally introduced to the lady my mother served. They had tea. My mother poured. I guess it was love at first sight." Vik picked up a leaf from the ground and slowly shredded it as he spoke. "Father came back from that year's campaign with a promotion and a medal and asked my mother to marry him. They had to get permission from Skandar, of course, and from the lady my mother served, but Father's outstanding record made that merely a formality. They had three months together. Then Father went off on another campaign."

"The one during which he deserted?"

"Yes. He found out his squadron was being sent on a suicide mission solely because of a bet between a lord and lady of the Council—the lady my mother served. She tried to make sure my mother knew nothing about it, but you can't keep secrets in one of those noble houses, not when the nobles tend to think of teks like furniture and say anything they feel like in front of them. My mother heard about the bet and warned my father. He left the Battlefield and disappeared. My mother was pregnant with me at the time." He tossed away the mangled remains of the leaf. "Three years later, a message found its way to my mother, to meet with other teks at an abandoned farm outside the city. Free Forcers met them there and escorted them to the valley. My father had built a house there for my mother...the house where I grew up. The house where my mother died, six months ago."

He fell silent. Kyla was still debating whether to prompt him with another question when he continued, in a voice barely audible. "She shouldn't have died. She only had the flu...if she'd stayed in Skandar, she'd still be alive. If my father had never deserted, all those people who died yesterday would still be alive."

Was this the source of his pain? "Not all of them," Kyla said. "The Free Forcers your father led off the Battlefield would have died on that suicide mission they'd been set up for. Your father might have died with them."

Vik said nothing.

"And the others...the others enjoyed fifteen years of freedom from Skandar and the Strator and nobles like the one your mother served." *Or the one I served.* "I only tasted three weeks of it, and I wouldn't give up those three weeks for a century-long lifespan as a tek servant. Tara was one of those who died. Would she have chosen to live if it meant living as a slave?"

"I don't know," Vik snarled. "My father didn't give her a choice. Just like he didn't give my mother a choice."

"She chose to go with him."

"Oh, they all chose to go with him...but none of them knew what it meant. None of them knew it would end in sickness and fire and death."

"But they knew it was a possibility. Vik, we never know for sure what the consequences of our choices will be. But we have to make those choices anyway. It's not fair to blame your father..."

"He promised to protect her! He promised to protect them all!" Vik shouted. He scrambled to his feet. "He couldn't. He lied!" And with that, he ran away, into the dark woods.

Kyla sighed. She heard Melodan coming up behind her. "What was that all about?" the pilot asked.

"Vik has just found out his father isn't perfect," Kyla said. "He's taking it hard."

"It's hard to take," Melodan said enigmatically and left her.

THE NEXT MORNING, Vik's shell seemed firmly in place again. Melodan ate a hard roll spread with soft cheese and listened as he unfolded their plan of attack. "We'll have help when we reach Skandar City," he explained. "One of our spies—the same one who told us Lady Moldar would be travelling into the mountains. She's going to hide us until we can meet with Kyla's brother."

Melodan stopped in mid-chew as a horrible thought occurred to her. She swallowed hastily. "Could she also have been the one who told Skyforce where to find the village?" she said.

Vik shrugged. "Yes. I don't believe she's the one who betrayed us—but there's no way to be sure."

"Wonderful."

A lone plane buzzed high overhead as they set out again, and Melodan thought uncomfortably of the Free Forcers, fleeing to the caves. Rand had put their lives in her hands—

but what if she failed? More people would die, and it would be her fault.

She remembered how she used to beg her father for more responsibility. Now she wasn't at all sure she liked it.

They made excellent time through the bands of trees that separated the tekfarms. With harvest complete, there were few people about. As the sun set, they reached the edge of the open space surrounding the city. Melodan stared across a sea of long grass, waving in a chill breeze, at the spaceport's high metal fence. The main control tower, her goal, rose even above the tall, old-fashioned gantries. But though it was only five kilometres or so away, it might as well have been five hundred. Even as she watched, three Skyforce planes roared in for a smooth landing on the vast field of blastrock.

As twilight deepened to night, Vik led the way around the city to a point where all the buildings they could see looked deserted. From his pack, he drew a flashlight and clicked it on-off, on-off, on-off.

A dim red flash answered him. "She's there," Vik whispered. "Let's go."

Together they dashed across the last hundred metres to Skandar City.

14 / THE SPACEPORT RAID

As they circled the city toward their rendezvous with Tor, Melodan moved up beside Kyla in the chill darkness. "What's wrong?" she asked quietly, pitching her voice so that Vik, bringing up the rear, would not hear her. Her breath made white clouds against the lights of Skandar.

"Nothing."

Melodan could only see Kyla's profile. "What did Tor tell you?"

"Leave me alone!" Kyla hurried forward, and Melodan let her go, wondering uneasily just what they would find at the fence.

And beyond it. Over and over, she had mentally rehearsed what she would have to do in the spaceport tower —but there were so many unknowns. How much time would she have? Skandar would know the moment she sent the message.

If it could be sent at all. There was no guarantee the transmitter still worked. But all she could do was try. As for what came after—

She looked at Kyla's stiff back. She had little hope any of them would escape. The moment Skandar detected the outgoing message, if not before, all hell would break loose. She wondered if Kyla realized that, if that was one reason for her hostility. *I'm putting her brother in danger, and I've already put her in danger*, Melodan thought. *Maybe she has a right to be hostile.*

It took most of their two hours to reach the far side of the spaceport. Hidden in the long grass, Melodan looked at the control tower, a hundred metres beyond the fence, rising from a cluster of lower buildings that hid Skybase. The fence and buildings alike were brightly lit, and Melodan wished for a moment fusion reactors did not last almost forever. A friendly shadow or two would have been welcome.

There were shadows aplenty beyond the tower, in the darkness of the vast landing apron, and Melodan watched them closely for movement.

"I don't like this," Vik said abruptly. "We've put our whole future in the hands of a Skyforce pilot."

"My brother," Kyla reminded him harshly.

"Maybe. But I've never heard of anyone deserting from Skyforce."

"Your entire Free Force deserted," Melodan pointed out.

"From Groundforce, not Skyforce." Vik's eyes flicked from side to side as he scanned the spaceport. Melodan glanced at Kyla, whose lips were pressed together. *She's worried, too*, she thought. *She's not as sure of her brother as she'd like to be. But why?*

She took a deep breath. If it was a trap, it was a trap. She had to play it out.

They waited.

In the robocab on the way back to Skybase, Tor leaned numbly against the cold glass of the window, watching the empty streets slide by.

He'd found no forgiveness, no absolution, in Kyla's eyes. She'd turned cold, as though the horror of what he'd confessed had frozen her very soul.

But if she could not yet forgive, at least she had offered him a means of redemption. The story she had told him—that the Preceptorate had returned and would soon take over the running of Avalon—sounded too preposterous to be true, but he didn't care why the Free Forcers needed to get into the spaceport. It was enough that they needed his help, that in some small way, he could make up for what he had done to them.

It would mean the end of his time in Skyforce, of course, but that must be near, anyway. Lady Moldar would soon tire of him and throw him like a bone to the Strator to try to ease her way back into the Council's good graces. And at this point, being thrown out of Skyforce would be more a relief than anything else.

The robocab delivered him to the Base gate, and the guards let him through with only a brief glance at his ID badge. He glanced at his watch. He had some equipment to gather and not much time in which to do so before the Free Forcers reached the rendezvous point near the spaceport control tower.

It took him longer than he expected. A cutter/welder was not an uncommon tool, but all equipment use was meticulously monitored in Skybase. Before he could gain access to a cutter, he had to convince the sergeant on duty in the quartermaster's office that he needed one. That involved fast talking, wholly imaginary damage to the ventilation system in his quarters, and the loss of the gold-plated steel Skyforce wings Lady Moldar had given him in place of the standard-issue silver-coloured plastic ones.

By the time he obtained the cutter, changed into an ordinary duty uniform from the dress uniform he had worn to Lady Moldar's, and dodged searchlights and sentries all the way across the spaceport to the rendezvous point, he was late.

He took one last look around from the shadow of the control tower, then dashed across the open space to the fence and crouched there. "Kyla?" he called softly through the plastic mesh.

Kyla rose from the grass, not five metres away. With were a boy, who must be the Vik she had told him about, and a young woman—the woman from the stars, if Kyla's story were true.

Vik carried a rifle that he kept aimed steadily at Tor. Tor held up his hands. "If you shoot me, how are you going to get through the fence?"

The young woman glanced at the boy. "Vik, please!"

Reluctantly, Vik lowered the weapon. It came back up again as Tor reached into one of the large pockets on his baggy navy-blue pants and drew out the pistol-shaped cutter, but finally went down and stayed down as Tor squeezed the cutter's trigger and the pointed tip of the barrel glowed white.

He touched it to the mesh of the fence. The acidcore plastic glowed and parted. Only a few drops of acid hissed on the blastrock; the cutter sealed off the strands at the same time as it sliced through them. In seconds, he'd made an opening large enough for the Free Forcers to crawl through.

Tor watched tensely as they straightened. Kyla, who had led the way, spoke first.

"You came," she said, her voice flat, almost hostile. Hearing that note in her voice hurt him more than anything that had gone before.

"You're my sister," he said softly.

Vik stepped impatiently forward. He did not offer to shake hands. "I'm Vik," he said. "I'm in command."

"I'm Melodan," said the young woman.

Tor looked at her. She looked ordinary enough. But then, what was he expecting—two heads? He nodded to her. "Follow me," he said.

Crouching low, they ran across the blastrock and into the narrow space between the tower and a lower building. "I don't think I set off an alarm on the fence, but entering the tower will activate one for sure," Tor said, pausing in the darkness. "We're a long way from the nearest guard post, but I don't think you'll have more than ten minutes inside. Possibly less. I hope that's enough."

"It will have to be," Melodan said.

"Then back out the fence?" said Vik.

"That may not be possible," Tor said. "They'll seal the perimeter first thing." He'd told Kyla all this. Hadn't she explained the dangers?

"As long as I do what I came to do," Melodan said grimly. "Getting out is secondary."

Well, she *knows what we're up against, anyway,* Tor thought approvingly. "Right. This way." The others followed him into a courtyard, surrounded by buildings on three sides. The fourth opened onto the landing field, where the lights of Skybase twinkled in the distance. Tor glanced that way. "No alarm yet," he said. "Shield your eyes."

He took out the cutter and twisted the handle, setting power output to maximum. The tip blazed like a miniature sun, throwing weird, elongated shadows from each of them across the courtyard. Squinting against the glare, Tor approached the tower's simple metal door—there was an astonishing amount of metal in the old spaceport buildings— and planted the glowing tip in the crack between door and doorpost. He squeezed the trigger.

Light streamed out around his hand as he slowly moved the cutter down the height of the door. Sparks and acrid smoke burst out as locking bolts were cut through—and off in the Skyforce compound, a siren wailed.

"Done," Tor said as he reached the bottom. "In more ways than one," he added, glancing toward the base. Then he put his shoulder to the door and pushed. It resisted only a moment before crashing open.

A corridor led deeper into the tower, and immediately to the left, stairs spiralled upward. Melodan pushed through the others, then turned to face them. "Stay here," she said. She hesitated, then held out her rifle to Tor.

He looked from it to Vik's glare. to Kyla's stony face, then took it from her. "Thanks," he said.

"If I'm not back before Skyforce gets here, you three will have to keep them out until I'm finished."

"You'll need this." Tor handed her the cutter.

She took it and started up the stairs.

With the others, Tor waited in silence broken only by the

wailing of the distant siren, like the first rumblings of thunder before the breaking of a storm.

———

THE STEPS SEEMED INTERMINABLE, but finally, Melodan reached the top landing, her heart thudding in her ears. A black door barred her way. Red-on-white letters proclaimed, "Main Control Emergency Exit. No Entry." The keyboard of an electronic lock blinked red in the wall to her right.

"Oh, yeah?" Melodan muttered and thrust the cutter against the keypad. There was a lick of flame and smoke, and the door slid open. To the accompaniment of shrilling alarms, Melodan stepped into the heart of the spaceport.

The air inside smelled stale and musty, with a hint of decay, but the tower still glowed with screens and lights. However, the archaic equipment was cluttered with unnecessary readouts and backup devices that made it difficult for Melodan to identify the particular console she needed. She began a slow circuit of the room, the alarm bells screaming in her ears, expecting at any moment to hear shots from below.

She almost passed over the controls she wanted: they were completely dark. Praying the emergency power systems still worked, she bent low over the console and flicked the necessary switch.

A new alarm sounded, a harsh clanging that made it hard to concentrate. Melodan did her best to ignore it. There could be no mistakes.

She began setting the dimspace relay frequencies, strings of numbers she had learned at the Academy—and complained about more than once. With the limited power of the ancient transmitter, she would have to relay the signal half a dozen times to get it to RSF Headquarters.

"Relay five: Barnard's Star," she muttered to herself. "And finally..." She entered the code for Headquarters and added the seven-letter combination that would give it such high priority it would practically jump out of the computer and scream for attention.

Then she reached for the keyboard. Time was slipping away. Skyforce guards would be there any moment. She activated the dimspace carrier wave and almost cheered as a green "READY TO TRANSMIT" appeared on the transmitter screen.

Swiftly but carefully, she typed, "PILOT FIRST CLASS MELODAN CASTILLE TO RSF. PRECEPTORATE REFORTIFYING AVALON. LOCAL FREEDOM FIGHTERS ENGAGED. REQUIRE IMMEDIATE ASSISTANCE." There was no time for more detail. Melodan added her ID code and hit TRANSMIT. A green light flashed, and the message was away—and so was she. She ran out the door and down the stairs. Kyla, Vik, and Tor all looked up as she descended. "Done," she said.

"I hear wheelers," Vik replied. "Let's get out of here."

They ran into the hostile night.

KYLA COULD HEAR THE WHEELERS, too, the whine of their engines growing closer. With the others, she dashed around the tower, back into the narrow passageway between the two buildings. But Tor stopped them abruptly before they reached the light. "Too late!"

The sound of engines came from both directions. Ovals of even brighter light swept over the floodlit pavement. "Trapped," growled Vik and swung his rifle toward Tor. "You set us up—"

Kyla pushed the rifle down. "Vik, don't. If we'd been set up, Melodan would never have been able to send her message."

"If it really went anywhere," Vik said. Kyla hadn't thought of that possibility; she wished he hadn't mentioned it.

"The equipment was working," Melodan said. "The message was sent."

Tor seemed to be ignoring the argument, all his attention on the wheelers, waiting to see where they appeared. When at last they swung into sight, loaded with armed men, he snapped, "This way!" and started back the way they had come.

Vik stayed where he was. "Go on," he said. "I'll be right behind you."

Kyla's heart jumped. She turned to argue, read the determination in Vik's eyes, and instead just touched his arm briefly before following Tor, who had hardly slowed at all, back into the courtyard. Shouts, then shots, echoed behind them as they clattered across the blastrock. "They've seen Vik!" Kyla cried, slowing and looking back.

"So, let's make sure they don't see us!" Tor pulled at her arm. "Run!" Kyla obeyed but kept looking back, and saw Vik emerge from between the two buildings, then turn and fire, the flame from his rifle lighting the dark passage.

They reached the deep shadow of a tall, skeleton-like gantry just as Vik began his lonely dash across the same bright pavement they had just traversed. Before he was halfway to them, Forcers swarmed from the gaps between the port buildings. "Stop!" someone shouted.

Vik kept running. Kyla started toward him, but Tor held her back, and an instant later, three sharp reports rang across the spaceport.

Vik's eyes jerked wide. His arms flew up, his rifle tumbling through the air and clattering on the pavement, and then he fell, sliding across the concrete to lie still and twisted.

Even across twenty metres, Kyla could see the dark, spreading stain on his back.

SOMEONE MOANED; it took Kyla a moment to realize it was her. Melodan's breathing was harsh and ragged, but Tor whispered, "He's bought us time. They'll think he was alone. And now I know how we're going to get out of here."

In that moment, Kyla's felt something for Tor again at last: pure, blinding hatred. She jumped at him, pummelling his chest with her fists, only the grief clogging her throat preventing her from screaming at him. He just stood there, taking it, until Melodan pulled her back. "There's no time for this!" Melodan whispered savagely in her ear. "Save it for later, when we're out of here!" Kyla kept struggling. Melodan shook her, hard. "Kyla, stop!"

She subsided, seething with fury and pain. "Where?" she heard Melodan ask Tor.

Tor pointed to another gantry several dozen metres distant and headed that way in a crouching run. The light pooled around the spaceport buildings didn't extend that far; he was all-but-invisible the moment he left their side.

Melodan took Kyla's arm. "Stay with us, Kyla," she said. "Don't dim out now."

Kyla shook her free. "I'm fine," she snarled. Her anger gave her strength. She followed her brother across the pavement, away from the Forcers surrounding Vik's motionless form, without even looking back.

Crouching in darkness beside the second gantry, Tor leaned close to Kyla and Melodan and whispered, "There's an entire squadron fuelled, armed, and waiting on the flight line. It's due to fly to the Battlefield tomorrow. I was supposed to be part of it." He took a deep, ragged breath. "We'll take one of the two-seater bombers."

"There are three of us," Melodan said.

"Two can ride in the bombardier's seat," he said tersely. "it won't be comfortable, but it's possible. With four it wouldn't have been."

Kyla wanted to hit him again but restrained herself.

Later, she thought. *Later, there'll be a reckoning.*

MELODAN STILL HADN'T REGAINED her breath when Tor led them off again, this time making no effort to be quiet or stay concealed, putting all his energy into speed. Melodan and Kyla trailed by five metres as he reached the nearest plane in a group of six lined up wingtip to wingtip in front of their hangars. He climbed into the back cockpit and pointed them to the front one. Kyla scrambled up first and settled herself, then Melodan sat down on her lap, hearing her grunt.

"We're heavy," Tor said as Melodan struggled to buckle

the unfamiliar harness over both of them. "We're going to need a long run to get airborne. We may get shot at. Then we have to make sure no one can follow us. See that bombsight?"

Melodan studied the panel before her. She had a duplicate set of flight controls, a cluster of navigation and communications instruments, and a small round screen with graduated crosshairs. "I see it."

"As we come back over the flight line I'll be strafing—that should knock out a few planes and keep the ground crews' heads down. We're carrying four racks of scatterfires. Once you see airplanes on the screen hit the red switches one after the other. Then hang on."

I hope we can, Melodan thought, pitying Kyla beneath her if they pulled any high-G manoeuvres. But there was nothing else to be done. "Ready?" she asked Kyla.

"Ready," Kyla said tightly, and Melodan suddenly remembered that Kyla was the only one of them who had never flown.

"You'll be all right," Melodan assured her, then raised her voice for Tor. "Let's do it."

"Right." The exhausts banged and belched blue fire and the engine exploded into raucous, throbbing life, rattling Melodan's teeth. The sweet smell of burning alcohol wafted over her.

The vibration eased as Tor cracked the throttle and they rolled slowly onto the runway and turned left. The lined-up squadron streamed past, then other parked aircraft, faster and faster, and despite everything, Melodan felt herself grinning hugely as the engine roared and wind reached for her around the tiny windscreen.

She felt the tail lift, but they were still on the ground, the end of the flight line rushing closer. Men appeared beyond the last plane, rifles flashing, and she ducked.

Then they were racing into the huge open space beyond the runway lights. *What a run-over area,* Melodan thought, *but it can't last forever...*

A gantry loomed ahead—

—and abruptly they were airborne, labouring upward into the night sky. The flashing red light that topped the gantry swept beneath their wings, and Melodan let out a breath she hadn't realized she was holding. The muscles of Kyla's legs were as hard as rocks beneath her, and she felt the other girl trembling.

Tor banked into a left-hand one-eighty, forcing Melodan uncomfortably down onto her seatmate's knees, and roared back toward the runway. Guns on the plane's nose blazed, tracers stitching fire across the ground, sending the men who had shot at them scrambling for cover.

A parked aircraft exploded in yellow fire and Melodan quickly looked down at the bombsight, now glowing blue. As the flaming wreckage swept into view, she flicked the bomb switches, one after the other.

The plane bucked, then soared. Melodan glanced back— and the world exploded.

Kyla screamed in her ear. Light and heat seared her eyes and scorched her face, and she gasped and jerked back into the cockpit. The plane pitched and yawed wildly, and she knew Tor had to be fighting a grim battle for control as the flames from bombs and bursting fuel tanks reached for them and shockwaves twisted fuselage and control surfaces to their limits.

She gasped air so hot it burned her lungs as a cloud of

black smoke laced with orange fire enveloped them and tossed them skyward, then suddenly, they were free of the inferno they had created, soaring smoothly into blessed coolness, the trailing edges of the wings redly reflecting the destruction behind them.

Melodan cautiously looked back down into a sea of fire. *I don't think anyone will be following us.* "You all right?" she shouted to Kyla.

Out of the corner of the eye, she saw the other girl nod, but she also heard something suspiciously like a sob, and felt Kyla's breast heave. At least, she hoped it was a sob, because if Kyla got airsick—

She almost dislocated her neck twisting around far enough to look at Tor, but he ignored her, his face set and grim.

Her own elation evaporated as she turned around again. She had succeeded—the Revolutionary Space Force was on the way, or soon would be.

But as she huddled in the cockpit, the chill of the night seeping in, she also thought of the cost.

Vik. The youngster she had never quite figured out—and now would never have the chance to. She thought of that last awkward parting of Vik and Rand and swallowed hard. She would have to bear the news to the Free Force commander. *Tara. Now Vik,* she thought. *How many more?*

Despite the roar of engine and wind, the silence was suddenly too much. She searched the controls again and found a microphone-headset. Settling it on her head, she asked, "Tor, can you hear me?"

After a moment of silence, his voice came back, devoid of inflection. "I hear you."

"Well—we did it."

Another pause. "Yes."

"Where are we going?"

"I'm taking you and Kyla to your Free Forcers."

"But we don't know where their hiding place is." A horrible thought struck her. "Do *you?*" If Tor knew where the caves were, then Skyforce knew, too!

"We're going to the valley. I can navigate there on instruments and drop flares to land."

Well, they'd already had painful evidence Skyforce knew where the valley was. "How much longer?"

"We're almost there."

She looked down, and saw they were already sweeping over the foothills. Ahead, she could see the peak, glittering with new snow, that rose above the Free Forcers' destroyed home.

A few minutes later, they began to descend. Something rattled beneath Melodan's feet and suddenly the valley blazed bright as day as flares drifted down on parachutes, their light amplified by the snow on the fields.

Tor banked toward a flat spot. "This could be rough," he warned.

It was. Frozen furrows beneath the snow bounced them high into the air and threatened to overturn them, and the jolt caused both Kyla and Melodan to gasp in pain. Again and again they crashed to ground and leaped back into the air, but each bounce was a little lower, and finally, they thumped across the last few metres and halted.

Melodan took a deep breath and somewhat shakily removed her headset. Tor could *fly*. She wondered what might have happened if she'd been at the controls.

At least I would have had a seat to myself, she thought, rubbing her bruised hip as she climbed from the cockpit. The flares burned out as she helped Kyla down beside her. Tor was already circling the aircraft, looking for damage. Then he glanced around. "Over there," he said, pointing to a copse of trees, black against the snow. "Cover."

"Why? You can't take off across this!" Melodan kicked at a furrow.

"You can't land on it, either." Tor grabbed a wing. "Help me push."

Melodan took the other wing and Kyla the tail, and together they forced the plane into the shelter of the trees. *A good hiding place*, Melodan thought. The plane's white wings and fuselage blended with the snow and the trees hid its telltale shape. It would be all-but-invisible from the air.

"We've got to rest," she said when at last the plane was hidden to Tor's satisfaction. "First light, we'll set out."

"Set out where?" an unexpected voice boomed from the bushes, and Melodan grabbed her rifle, then froze as two armed men, heavily swathed in fur, stepped into the moonlight. "Skyforce spies aren't welcome around here."

RAND LOOKED across the large central cavern they called the Great Hall, thick with sweet smoke from the fires burning around its circumference and at its centre despite the crevices that formed natural chimneys in the stalactite-hung ceiling. He heard the low murmur of conversation, but not much of it. The Free Forcers were tired: tired, dispirited, and cold. Winter had come early. They'd found little game so far in the valleys surrounding the barren peak beneath which they hid. The only good thing was that the snow should have wiped out whatever trail they might have left for Ground-force...but it wouldn't do a thing to stop hunger from finding them when the food ran out, as it surely would, in a few weeks—or a few days.

The two-day journey to the caves had been hellish. They'd lost five more people, four of them wounded in the Skyforce attack, one of them a little boy who fell as they were traversing a slippery mountain ledge. *More deaths to my account*, he thought.

He wondered if Melodan had succeeded. They knew the raiding party had arrived; Hildar had informed them of that much. By now, the attempt to infiltrate the spaceport must have been made. He didn't suppose they'd know what had happened until either the Preceptorate or the Revolutionary Space Force—or both—appeared in their skies.

If any of them were still alive by then.

He shook his head and walked toward the largest tunnel leading to the surface, the main entrance into the cave system. He had to shake off this depression—*had* to, for the Free Forcers' sake. He knew how much his own black mood could further erode already shaky morale. People in desperate straits didn't want to see their leader walking around like a zombie, like a man who had given up on living.

Even if that was what he was becoming.

Halfway up the tunnel, he met Wan, one of the sentries, coming down. "Radio message from Starax," Wan said. "From the valley."

More bad news? Rand thought wearily. He followed Wan up the rough, sloping tunnel to the shale-strewn entrance. The other sentry on duty there, a woman named Nell, silently handed him one of the communicators Hildar had smuggled to them aboard Lady Moldar's wheelers. "Rand here," he said.

"A Skyforce plane just landed in the valley, Colonel," Starax said. "But you'll never guess who was aboard it..."

He was in no mood for guessing games. "Starax, report!" he snapped—but it wasn't Starax who replied.

"Hello, Colonel," said a woman's voice.

Rand exchanged startled glances with Wan. "Melodan? How did you...?"

"Kyla's brother flew us out in a Skyforce plane," her voice crackled back. "Rand, I sent the message. It's only a matter of days before help arrives."

Days. How many days? She couldn't tell him, of course; no use asking. "Even one day is a long time up here, Melodan, but we'll do our best." He paused. "Is Vik with you?"

Silence.

"Melodan?" He checked the communicator. The green light was still on. "Repeat, is Vik with you?"

Her voice, when it came again, sounded strained. "No, Colonel. He's—he was shot."

Rand stared at the communicator. He felt numb. One more blow, the biggest of all...too big. Too big to feel. His ocean of pain had long ago crept over the shore; now there seemed to be no land left anywhere left to cling to. "Come to the caves as soon as you can," he heard himself say. "Out." He turned and handed the communicator to Wan, then walked away from the cave entrance into the darkness.

He wondered if it would ever be light again.

ARTEGA STOOD over the wounded Free Forcer boy, who lay bound to the plastic rails of the hospital bed by stout straps of braided black synthetic. The boy's eyes, startlingly blue in his pale face, stared resolutely at the glowing light panel overhead.

The Strator glanced at the white-coated man watching lights and blue worm-crawls on the bedside monitor. "Well?"

"I think he's strong enough now," the man replied stiffly. "But I am still against it."

"Fortunately, Dr. Methon, it is not your decision." Artega turned back to the boy. "I have some questions for you."

"I've got nothing to say." The boy's voice was hoarse but fierce.

"You have no choice. Doctor?"

Stonily, the doctor lifted a syringe from a tray of instruments by the bed. He removed the protective cap from the ceramic needle and squirted pale green liquid into the air. The boy watched warily as the needle approached his arm and winced as it stabbed home. Then his eyes widened abruptly before dropping closed. His chest began to rise and fall rapidly.

The doctor nodded to Artega and stepped back.

"Can you hear me?" Artega said.

"Yes," the boy whispered.

"What is your name?"

"Vik."

"Vik, there is something I need to know that only you can tell me. Will you help me?"

"Yes."

"Vik, the Free Forcers fled their valley, didn't they?"

"Yes."

Artega leaned a little closer. "Where did they go?"

Vik frowned slightly, but he replied clearly, "The caves."

"Where are these caves, Vik?"

The boy's frown deepened. The monitor beeped. "His heart rate is elevated," the doctor said. "He's fighting it."

Artega leaned closer. "You promised to help me, Vik. Remember?"

"Yes..."

"Where are the caves?"

The boy's chest heaved. The monitor beeped again, more insistently. "Can't..."

"Yes, you can, Vik. Where are the caves?"

Vik's hands gripped the sheet. His eyes fluttered. The monitor's beeping became constant.

The doctor glared at Artega. "Do you want to kill him?"

"Quiet!" Artega snapped. "Tell me, Vik! *Where are the caves?*"

The boy's mouth opened—closed—opened again. Word by slow word he choked out, "Forty...kilometres...southwest!"

"Thank you." Artega stepped back smugly. "He's all yours, doctor."

At once the doctor plunged a second syringe into Vik's arm, and slowly his struggling ceased, until he lay at rest, sweat beading his forehead and chest. Artega waited until Vik's eyes opened and met his. "You were very helpful," he said and, filled with the satisfaction of seeing the boy's horror, left the room.

His good feeling lasted only back to his office, where he found two messages waiting—one from the commander of Skybase and one from Baron Markus.

Knowing he wouldn't like what Markus had to say, he called the Skyforce commander first. "Report," he snapped as the man appeared, his florid face mottled, his neck red and bulging above his blue collar.

What he heard did nothing to improve his rapidly souring mood. The brother of the traitor Kyla—for there could be no doubt who was responsible—had been depressingly thorough in removing the threat of pursuit the evening before. The parked aircraft had been easy targets, lined up along the runway. No precautions against attack had been taken. Fighting took place only on the Battlefield, between drafted teks, not where lords and ladies could be endangered.

As a result, no serviceable planes remained of the Base's complement of thirty, and only half a dozen could even be repaired. Which meant Artega's only active aircraft were those on the Battlefield.

After the commander signed off, Artega stared at the

blank vidscreen a moment longer, gathering his wits and his emotions. He needed complete control before confronting Baron Markus.

At last, he keyed "accept."

Markus appeared at once. "Artega, you fool," he said coldly. "The Preceptor will skin you alive."

Artega felt his anger rising. "I warned you these Free Forcers were a threat," he snapped back. "You refused to give me what I needed to crush them. Now this Rebel scout *you* let slip through your fingers has warned your enemies. I think the Preceptor may have a few choice words for you, too!" He saw Markus's eyes flicker and knew he'd scored. He pressed on. "Now, I ask you again for help in eliminating them. I've learned where they've retreated to—"

But Markus's momentary discomfiture had vanished. He smiled viciously. "My dear Strator, it is hardly of any use now, is it? The damage is done. The Free Forcers do not threaten the Preceptorate—only your control. I will come to Avalon only as escort to the Preceptor—not before." His lips drew back further, exposing his teeth. "I expect that to occur within days. So, don't count on the arrival of the rebels to rescue you from the Preceptor's wrath. Once he is here and activates the planetary defences, as he intends to do personally, he will have plenty of leisure to deal with *you*. Markus out."

The screen went blank.

Artega very slowly unclenched his fists. "Skandar."

"Yes, Strator?"

Artega felt fiercer pleasure than usual at the AI's obedience. *The Preceptor still needs Skandar, and that means he still needs me*, he thought tauntingly at the distant Markus. *We'll see which of us is of more value.*

"Awaiting instructions, Strator," Skandar reminded him, and he wrenched his mind back to the present.

Skyforce can't do the job alone, he thought. Even in the valley it hadn't been able to. The Free Forcers had managed to flee before Groundforce arrived, and then the damned snow had destroyed any hope of tracking them.

He steepled his fingers as he thought. *This time, Skyforce and Groundforce must attack simultaneously.* And that meant he would have to pull troops and aircraft from the Battlefield, even if it meant taking losses there.

He grinned savagely. Let the other cities celebrate victories over Skandar for a few days. Skandar would rule supreme when the Preceptor made it his capital. "Contact the Battlefield commanders," he told Skandar. "New orders."

"Yes, Strator."

Artega leaned back in his chair, tapping his forefingers together. *I'm still in control*, he thought. *And I'm going to stay that way.*

***

MELODAN and the others spent the night huddled around an inadequate fire. Beyond the leaping flames, Melodan could see Kyla's pale face, the fire reflecting sparks from her eyes as she stared into it blankly. The younger girl had hardly spoken since Vik was shot; she and her brother had barely glanced at each other.

Melodan shook her head. "How long?" she asked Tor abruptly.

He didn't ask what she meant. "I doubt there are more than two or three planes still usable at Skybase," he said. "The Strator will have to order some away from the Battlefield, and he can't do that quickly without risking major defeat. I'd say we're safe from attack for at least three days. But there may be scouting flyovers."

Melodan glanced at the shifting patterns of firelight on the plane's white fuselage. "How much fuel left?"

"A few hours."

"We need it close to the caves if it's going to be any use."

"There's no place to land up there," Starax objected.

"We'll make one," Melodan said. "My people are at least ten days away. We can't count on the caves remaining secure all that time."

"Skandar's Forcers couldn't find us fifteen years ago," Starax argued. "The Strator can't want our blood any more now than he did when we deserted."

"You didn't see what we did to Skybase." Melodan looked at Tor again. "How many planes could he pull off the Battlefield?"

"I'm not sure—maybe half a dozen."

"Six against one. Think you're up to it?"

He looked away.

Melodan poked at the fire, frowning. There was something in his eyes, the way he spoke, that reminded her...

...reminded her of a pilot her father had brought home with him once for a six-day leave, who had the same drawn look and dead tone. Late one night, she'd overheard her father telling her mother, "I'd hoped to snap him out of it— but it's not working."

"What happened to him?" Melodan's mother had asked.

"His wingman cut in front of him during a dogfight. His beams killed his best friend." And then he had said, "He doesn't much care about living anymore, Vella. And pilots who don't worry about staying alive usually don't."

Two weeks later, the pilot died in a minor skirmish over an obscure planet.

Melodan cleared her throat. "There's one other thing."

Tor looked up.

"You can't do all the flying. You'll have to teach me."

He blinked, and Melodan thought she saw the corner of his mouth twitch with the faintest beginning of a smile. "That should be...interesting," he said.

———

At dawn, with their breath making great clouds in the crisp mountain air, Starax led Melodan, Tor, and Kyla out of the valley, promising the Free Forcer they left behind that he would soon be relieved. "It took Rand and the others two days to make the trip to the caves," Starax said as they set out. "But they had children and wounded and a lot of baggage to worry about. We should be able to make it in one." He grinned. "A *long* one."

Melodan groaned.

They turned south, then west, climbing steadily toward peaks turned golden by the rising sun.

Melodan's body was warm, so warm that beads of sweat formed on her forehead, where they burned like fire as the wind tried to turn them to ice, but frozen vises seemed to clamp her fingers and toes, and the cold made her face and jaw so stiff she could hardly talk. For a time, she worried about frostbite, but the telltale white patches of frozen skin never appeared. Her fingers remained an angry red, until she almost wished they *would* freeze, just a little, so she wouldn't feel them quite so much.

They warmed finally as the sun climbed higher, and soon the snow, while in no danger of melting away completely, was at least shrinking in on itself and glistening wetly instead of glittering diamond-hard.

They stopped for a few minutes each hour and paused half an hour for a midday meal, but otherwise hiked steadily upward, leaving even the trees behind them as the afternoon wore on. Kyla remained as silent as she had the day before, and for her part, Melodan preferred to save her breath for climbing. Tor stayed a little apart from the other three and didn't speak, either.

A massive peak of basalt, a dimensionless black cutout against the setting sun, loomed ahead of them when Starax abruptly veered north up a slope of loose stone toward a ridge crowned with enormous rocks like broken teeth. Melodan followed slowly on sore feet and chilled limbs, too tired to even ask how near they were to their goal.

Then they crested the slope and she looked into the Free Forcers' caves.

Too much had happened in too short a time. Kyla couldn't process it emotionally anymore. Learning Tor had participated in the attack on the valley, seeing Vik get shot, the terror of their flight from Skybase, and then the long, grinding climb to this place...Kyla's face and toes were numb with cold, but no more numb than her soul.

She stared at the entrance to the caves. The fang-like rocks that crowned the ridge had fallen from cliffs higher up the mountain, tumbling off an overhanging shelf beneath which were three dark openings. Rand was shaking hands with Starax, talking to him earnestly. Behind them, dim figures moved about, silhouetted against red fire-glow.

Rand seemed to have aged years in the few days they had been separated, his face etched by new worry and pain. He greeted Kyla and Melodan gravely, then held out his hand as Tor joined them. "Thank you—" he began.

Tor turned and walked away.

Rand looked at Kyla. "Kyla?"

"I'm sorry, Colonel," she said. "Tor is..." *A murderer? A*

butcher? "...confused. It hasn't been...easy for him." *Why are you defending him? a part of her yelled. Tell them the truth. Tell them what he did!*

But, somehow, she couldn't.

Without another word, she brushed past Rand and fled inside.

———

RAND STARED AFTER KYLA, then turned to Melodan. "I hope you're not going to run away the moment I start talking to you, as well," he said.

"No, Colonel," Melodan said. "I apologize. I don't know what's wrong with either one of them. Tor I can sort of understand—he must feel like a traitor to everyone—but Kyla has been acting strangely since she first spoke to Tor, and I don't know why." She shrugged. "But they saved us all."

"Not all," Rand said. His throat closed off and he had to swallow to speak again. He sat wearily on a nearby rock. He felt tired all the time, these days, more tired than a man his age ought to feel. "We had a visitor earlier. A single Skyforce plane." He had been called to the surface to see it as it flew over, so high their rockets couldn't touch it—Skyforce had learned that lesson well. The buzz of its engine had echoed mockingly from the rocky peaks around them.

"Did the pilot spot you?" Melodan asked anxiously.

"I don't think so. But he didn't have to. He wasn't just scouting; he had come to this spot, specifically." He bent over, picked up a pebble, and flung it into the darkness. A second later, it clattered on the rocks downslope.

"Then Skyforce knows where we are! But how?"

Rand shook his head. "I don't know."

Melodan sat beside him on a boulder. "So, what happens next?"

You tell me, Rand thought. *You're the one who promised we'd be saved by an army from outer space.* His own bitterness surprised him. "We'll be attacked. And by more than just Skyforce." Rand pointed west, toward the basalt peak. "I expect Groundforcers from the Battlefield to come marching through the pass north of that peak."

"How soon?"

"Ten days, if we're lucky." That's how long it had taken his deserters to make the trip fifteen years ago, slowed down by wounded. "A week if we're not." Blackness was chasing the last grey light from the sky. An icy breeze swept down from the peak. Rand looked at Melodan again. "But you tell me we must hang on for two weeks."

Melodan managed a small smile. "Ten days if we're lucky."

Rand snorted. "So. Fifteen years of hiding, of striking at the Strator and Skandar when we could, fifteen years of trying to live free—and it all comes down to who gets here first."

Melodan rubbed her arms for warmth. "It's hasn't been for nothing, Rand," she said, her voice almost pleading, and he wondered if she were trying to convince him or herself. "The RSF has been warned that the Preceptorate is here and will know the Preceptor is on his way. It has to get here first. That's the race that matters. If the RSF succeeds, it will be because of us. Whether we're alive or dead."

It was the very argument Rand had been using on himself to alleviate the gnawing guilt he felt over all those who had died. So far, it hadn't worked. "Fatalism from one so young?"

Melodan's smile returned. "Actually, that was just a modified version of a standard speech they used to give us at the Academy."

Rand snorted. "The Battlefield commanders say similar things. It may be true, but it's not very comforting." He climbed heavily to his feet and held out his hand to help her up. "Come on inside and tell everyone your story. A little hope is better than no hope at all."

At least she can offer the Free Forcers that, he thought. He no longer could; it was hard to give someone else something he had long since lost himself.

OVER THE NEXT FEW DAYS, Melodan helped the Free Forcers prepare their defences. The caves were naturally fortified by the fallen rock in front of the three tunnel entrances and the loose scree on the slope. Together, they would make a frontal assault almost suicidal—as long as the defenders' ammunition held out.

Heavy artillery could have reduced the cave openings to rubble, trapping the Free Forcers inside, but heavy artillery didn't exist on Avalon, Meloidan had learned. The most powerful weapons Groundforce could bring to bear would be hand-launched missiles like the ones Melodan had already seen bring down Skyforce planes, and the Free Forcers had their own stock of those.

However, Rand was not content to sit and wait for the attack, and neither was Melodan. While he sent fighters to the pass to prepare booby-traps, she supervised the levelling of a stretch of ground at the base of the slope below the caves. Though Tor remained stand-offish around the Free Forcers, she managed to draw him into the work: she had to, since he was the only one who knew how long and how smooth the runway had to be.

The length was limited by the small expanse of flattish land, but when it was finished after three days of hard work, helped by a return to warm weather, Tor said that he thought it might be usable, "If we're lucky."

"We're already depending so much on luck, a little more won't hurt," Melodan said wryly.

Kyla posed a more difficult problem. Part of the time she seemed like her old self, at least around Melodan and other Free Forcers, but whenever Tor came near, she withdrew. Something had happened between her and her brother, Melodan could tell, but she didn't know what—and the pace of preparation for attack precluded trying to find out. Personal problems would have to wait until later.

If there *were* a later.

Just before noon on the fourth day after arriving at the caves, Melodan and Tor set out for the valley again. Kyla watched them go, but though she waved good-bye to Melodan, when Tor glanced back, she turned away. Melodan looked at Tor's grim face and decided not to ask any questions.

They made better time than they had on the uphill journey, aided by the warmer weather as well as the downward slope, and reached the valley soon after nightfall, while some light still lingered over the Skandar plain.

The man guarding their "air force" greeted them enthusiastically, especially when Melodan gave him Rand's orders. "When we take off tomorrow, Rand wants you back at the caves. Once the plane is gone there'll be no reason to stay."

He wanted to know a thousand things about the defensive preparations, and Melodan's hope of speaking privately to Tor before morning was lost in his chatter. By the time they turned in, Tor was already asleep, back to the fire, and her own questions were left unanswered.

At first light, she helped Tor roll the plane into the open. He knelt and felt the ground. "It's terribly soft," he said to Melodan. "It was frozen when we landed. If we bog down..."

"We'll dig it out and start over," Melodan said firmly. "Now, are you going to fly, or shall I?"

She was rewarded with a rare smile. "Think you could?"

"Why not?" After all, she thought, the principles of atmospheric flight were the same in a wooden biplane as in a duratitanium-hulled spaceplane.

Tor, however, seemed unwilling to let her prove it just yet. "Once we're airborne, you can take the stick," he said. "But *I'll* get her in the air."

I hope so, Melodan thought as she climbed into the front cockpit and saw just how deeply the wheels had sunk into the soft ground. What had been a snow-covered field was now a quagmire of scorched earth, ash, and blackened stubble. *Never thought I'd wish it were freezing cold after that climb to the caves.*

Tor fired the engine and they started to roll. Slowly, slowly they picked up speed, weaving and skidding in the mud, while the row of trees ahead of them seemed to double in size every second. *We'll never make it*, Melodan thought.

We'll never— "We'll never make it!" she shouted into her headset.

Tor said nothing, but the engine thundered, the ailerons went down, and ponderously, like a giant bird struggling up from flat ground, the plane tugged free of the grasping mud, staggered in mid-air, then suddenly soared.

The tops of the trees swept beneath the wings—but not by much. "You were saying?" Tor said, and Melodan laughed. Then, after they had gained more altitude, he asked, "Ready to take her?"

Melodan nodded, realized he couldn't see her, and said out loud, "Ready," as she grasped the stick. An instant later, she was no longer a passenger but the pilot.

Until then she hadn't known how much she missed flying. But suddenly, she felt in complete control for the first time in a long time.

She pulled back sharply and the nose pitched up. At once, a light blinked red and something buzzed in her ear—clearly a stall warning—and then the aircraft nosed down. As the airspeed indicator climbed again, she regained control, but the plane pitched up and down, in smaller and smaller increments, five or six times.

She swallowed. Her exhilaration had given way to faint nausea.

"Interesting technique," Tor remarked.

"It's not as easy as I thought," Melodan admitted. "Do you want her back?"

"No, you go ahead. You know what you're doing; you just need practice."

"You can say that again," she muttered.

As they flew on, she tried less violent manoeuvres and

soon began to get a feel for the plane. With neither the structural strength or overwhelming engine power of a spaceplane, it could not perform the high-G turns, dives, and rolls she had learned. But it was surprisingly nimble in some ways, turning in amazingly little airspace and responding lightly to her touch on stick and pedals.

"I think I'm beginning to—" Melodan started to say, then felt the stick go dead in her hand as Tor took back control. "What—?"

She got no further. Tor flung the plane violently left as tracers ripped a double row of holes in the wing above her head.

THE STRUGGLE TO get the plane into the air, the triumph as it lifted over the trees, the simple joy of flying...all those things had temporarily lifted Tor out of himself, so that, as he coached Melodan on the biplane's controls, he was almost happy. He even relaxed enough to stop the constant head-swivelling search of the sky he'd had drilled into him since his first day of Skyforce training.

It almost got them killed. Only by chance did he glance over his shoulder and see the black speck of another plane dropping out of the sky toward them.

He deactivated Melodan's stick, grabbed his own, and shoved it forward, diving for speed. You wanted altitude in a dogfight. If you couldn't get altitude, you went for speed, headed for the deck, and hoped your attacker was unwilling to follow. A burst of tracers chased them, tearing holes in the fuselage and wings—but then their attacker swept overhead and kept on going.

Tor levelled off only fifty or sixty metres above the treetops. "Why didn't he stay to fight?" Melodan asked in his headphones.

"Low on fuel," Tor said shortly. Ahead, he could see more black specks, circling the peak that hid the caves. "Let's hope they all are."

Apparently, they were. The Skyforcers fled east as Melodan and Tor approached. "They've been here a while," said Tor. "I hope we still have a place to land."

Melodan looked out and down. "The strip looks intact. But there's fighting near it. Just a skirmish, no large force."

Tor glanced over the side. Groundforcers crouched behind rocks up the slope from the landing strip. His hand tightened on the stick. For a moment he saw other Forcers crouched behind rocks, on a mountain slope beside the wreckage of a mysterious vessel, and watched Parl's plane explode in mid-air...

...and then he remembered men and women in a wheat-field falling beneath his guns.

"Maybe we can help," Melodan said. "A strafing run?"

A single pass would break up the skirmish, Tor thought. But the thought of watching more people die at his hand... "No. I...I can't."

"Then let me," Melodan snapped.

"No!"

"If we try to land while those Groundforcers are lurking by the strip, they'll shoot us out of the air. We've got to clear them out." A pause. "You've cast your lot with the Free Forcers, Tor. It's too late to back out now."

She was right, of course. Tor knew it. He'd betrayed his sister by letting himself be pulled into Skyforce, betrayed his best friend by letting go of his pledge of vengeance for his death, and betrayed his oath to Skyforce by attacking his own base. He'd broken every promise and every commitment he'd ever made and ended up back where he should have stayed, with Kyla, on the side of the teks. If he betrayed her again, he'd lose her forever. And he had nothing and no one else to live for.

Without another word, he banked the plane and dived toward the valley.

Puffs of dust and shattered rock raced across the slope where the Groundforcers crouched. Several fell. Others ran. A few held their ground and fired back, but as Tor swung around for a second pass, they, too, scrambled away.

Feeling no exhilaration, only fatigue and bitterness, Tor landed moments later, the plane rolling to a halt only three or four metres from the end of the tiny strip. Jubilant Free Forcers surrounded them. "Sent 'em running back where they came from!" said one. "They didn't expect us to have our own Skyforce!"

"When did they attack?" Melodan asked as she climbed from the cockpit.

"Around noon," said a woman whose arm was bound in a bloody rag. "They picked away at us for an hour or two, then the planes came over and dropped bombs. Didn't do much damage. Didn't stay long, either."

"They must have flown all the way from the Battlefield," Tor said tiredly. "They only had enough fuel to stay over the target for a few minutes."

"We have to talk to Rand," Melodan said to him.

The last person Tor wanted to see was the colonel. "You go. I'll look after the plane."

"No. Both of us." She grabbed his shoulder, turning him

to face her. "I don't know what your problem is, but we can't afford it anymore! We need what you know about the Forcers. *You have to talk to Rand.*"

Tor slowly ran his finger along the plane's wing, from bullet hole to bullet hole. "These need patching," he said. "But I guess they'll wait." Abruptly he turned toward her. "All right."

They found Rand at the cave entrance, talking to a man and a woman. He turned toward Tor and Melodan, looking grim. "A large force is coming this way," he said. "I doubt we can hold it off for more than a few hours—maybe a day." He looked hard at Melodan. "Will your people come within the next two days?"

"I don't know," she said. "I hope so."

"Hope won't stop Groundforce."

"The plane might," Tor said. He heard his own words with surprise. "Hit them *before* they reach the pass."

Rand raised an eyebrow at him. "You couldn't do much damage against a force that size."

"But they'd have to take cover. It would slow them down, at least—buy some time."

Rand nodded. "Good thinking, lad." He held out his hand. "Now will you shake it?"

Your latest oath of commitment, Tor thought, looking down at the colonel's hand. *How long before you betray this one?*

He shook Rand's hand briefly, then pulled free and turned away.

"Sir!" A lookout hurried over, binoculars in hand. "Two snipers coming down the far slope!"

Rand took the glasses and studied the other side of the

ravine. "Artan!"

The Free Forcer Rand had been talking to earlier stepped forward. "Yes, Colonel?"

"Warn them down below."

"Yes, sir!"

Artan plunged down the slope. Tor studied the far slope. Without binoculars, and in the fading light, he couldn't see the snipers. But then his gaze wandered right, and he suddenly cried, "No!"

A boy no more than ten was picking his way downhill, eyes fixed on the plane. Melodan started forward, but Rand grabbed her arm. "Artan, behind you!" Rand shouted. The young man looked up, skidded to a halt, and started scrambling toward the boy—

—AND THE SNIPERS OPENED FIRE.

A bullet ricocheted off a nearby rock, sending Rand and Melodan scrambling for cover. But Tor ignored it. Eyes fixed on the boy, he plunged downhill.

The boy had stopped, frozen. Another bullet cracked off stone at his feet. A fragment of rock stung Tor's face as he half-ran, half-slid down the slope, the rocks shifting treacherously beneath him. He could slip and break a leg at any moment...but then he reached the child and scooped him up in his arms.

He turned to run back up the slope, but before he'd taken a step something slammed into his back with a force so great it was beyond pain, smashing him to the ground, the boy beneath him. Through ringing ears, he thought he heard Melodan scream his name.

I guess I won't betray anyone again was his last thought as the darkness took him.

———

Kyla, who had been ordered to take cover in the caves during the Skyforce attack and the skirmish with Ground-force, heard the plane land, but though she very much wanted to see Melodan, she didn't go out to meet it. Meeting it as soon as it landed would mean meeting Tor, too.

Sooner or later, they would have to talk, would have to reach some kind of understanding...but she didn't know what good it would do. How could she ever understand why Tor had attacked the valley, slaughtering people she'd begun to count as her friends and family? How could she ever forgive him, no matter how much Tor did to help them now?

Maybe time would help ease things between them, but if so, it would take more than the few days that had passed since she'd found out the truth.

Still, she wanted to see Melodan, and so after several minutes, she made her way toward the cave entrance, expecting to see her friend coming in. Halfway there, she was passed by a small boy, who almost knocked her over in his eagerness to get outside. "We've got an airplane!" he shouted over his shoulder to her as he ran past, and she smiled after him.

She was surprised to see twilight outside; she'd lost track of time in the caves, not the first time that had happened.

As she reached the entrance, she saw the boy who had passed her in the tunnel starting carefully down the slope that led to the landing strip, no doubt to get a closer look at the airplane. Off to her left, Melodan stood talking with Rand, a few other Free Forcers...and Tor. Kyla hung back, silently willing her brother to go away.

There was a sudden flurry of activity, people pointing into the ravine. Artan scrambled out of sight.

Gunshots! Kyla shrank back against the cave wall. Outside, people shouted, and sudden horror seized her heart as she remembered the boy. As she started forward, ready to scream a warning, she saw Tor plunging out of sight into the ravine.

Crouching low, she zig-zagged across the ledge to the safety of a boulder. Raising up a little, she looked downslope—

—just in time to see Tor, the terrified boy in his arms, crumple to the ground.

Even in the fading light she could see dark blood soaking his back.

Just like Vik.

The child Tor had saved scrambled up, unhurt, and fled, wailing, back to the caves.

Down below, Free Forcers opened up on the snipers' positions. No more bullets crossed the ravine. Kyla scrambled out of hiding and ran to her brother.

Tor lay with his head turned awkwardly, his cheek pressed to the stones, his breath coming in shallow, bubbling gasps. Blood trickled from his mouth, and his eyes, half-closed, flickered wildly.

Melodan, Rand, and others reached them. A medic knelt beside Tor. "He's dying!" Kyla said wildly. *Dying.* Her thoughts echoed through her shock and confusion. *Dying! And we haven't...I haven't...*

"He's not dead yet," Melodan said, pulling her gently to her feet. "Let the medic work."

Kyla hardly heard her. "Shot," she whispered. "Just like Vik."

She heard Rand's sharp intake of breath and regretted her words. Then the colonel spoke, his voice steady but immensely weary. "I was just beginning to trust him," he said softly.

The medic stood. "We have to get him inside!"

"Is it safe to move him?"

"Safer than leaving him here," the medic snapped. "I have better equipment inside. Let's go!"

Kyla wrenched free of Melodan and returned to Tor's side, holding his hand as the Free Forcers carefully carried him up the slope, leaving a trail of blood.

Inside, the medic had Tor taken into the chamber they had designated the infirmary and ordered Kyla to stay outside. She leaned back against the rough stone wall, slid slowly to the cold stone floor, and waited.

She had things to say to Tor. She needed answers. She needed to understand...

Now, she might never get the chance.

* * *

MELODAN SAT BESIDE HER FRIEND. Kyla's face had thinned considerably since she'd first joined the Free Forcers. Here and now, in the flickering light of the torches that lit this part of the cave, she looked positively gaunt, and far older than her age.

Melodan doubted she looked any better.

She'd spoken privately to the medic after her ordered Kyla out of the infirmary, before she'd followed. He hadn't been encouraging. "In the hospital in Skandar he might have a chance. But here?" He'd shrugged.

"He's dying, isn't he?" Kyla said suddenly.

Melodan couldn't lie to her. "Yes." She took Kyla's hand. "Kyla, I'm sorry. I'm responsible. I got Tor involved in all this."

Kyla shook her head. "No. *I* talked him into helping us. And...maybe it's for the best. Maybe better this than..." Her voice trailed off.

"What's wrong between you two?" Melodan asked after a moment.

Kyla pulled her hand away and looked down. "Nothing."

"Ever since that night in Skandar, you've practically been sleepwalking. I thought it was shock—Vik—" Melodan swallowed. "But that's not all, is it?"

Slowly Kyla looked up. "No," she whispered. "Melodan, I told you about my first meeting with Tor—how he didn't want to leave Skyforce. The second time, in Lady Moldar's townhouse—the second time was worse. Melodan—he was with the Skyforcers that day. *He was one of those who destroyed the village!*"

Melodan felt as if a bucket of icewater had been upended over her head. For a moment she couldn't breathe. "Are you sure?" she whispered at last.

"He admitted it! Melodan, he was one of those who attacked the Free Forcers the day they found you, too. That Skyforcer that Skandar shot down was Tor's best friend. He *wanted* to take part in the attack on the village. He wanted revenge." She folded her arms, hunched over as though warding off a cold rain. "When he told me that...all of a sudden, he didn't seem like my brother anymore. He was a stranger who might do anything—lie to me, betray me, kill me.

"But I knew he was our only hope of getting into the spaceport—the only hope for the Free Forcers. So I bet my life, all of our lives, that there was something left of my brother inside that horrible uniform. I told him the only way he could make up a little for what he'd done was to let us into the spaceport.

"But even after he got us through the fence and flew us to safety, I doubted him. The brother I knew back on the tekfarm could never have done what Skyforce did to the village. He still seemed like a stranger to me, so I avoided him. Now—" Her voice broke; she paused and swallowed. "Now I may never have the chance to get to know him again."

Melodan had no comfort to offer. She hugged Kyla to her, and they clung there until the medic came to the door of the cavern.

He offered no hope. Tor might linger for hours, but without proper hospital treatment, his chance of survival was practically nil.

Kyla got to her feet. Tears still stained her face. "I'd like to sit with him," she whispered. "If I may."

Without a word, the medic led her into the infirmary.

Melodan rubbed her own eyes with the back of her hand, then made her solitary way to her sleeping roll.

In the morning, Tor still lived, barely. Kyla had fallen asleep beside him, Melodan saw when she visited the infirmary. She didn't disturb her. Instead, she returned to the cave mouth and watched daylight grow, taking deep breaths of the crisp morning air. *It's light enough,* she thought. *Groundforce will be marching.*

She knew she would have fly the plane if the Free Forcers were to have any hope of survival. But what could she do against five Skyforcers or more?

I'm a good pilot. Give me time to learn the machine and I'll prove it.

But time was in short supply—for everyone.

Rand joined her. "The main force will be in position to attack by dawn tomorrow," he said, looking down at the white cruciform shape of their aircraft. "Today, I think they'll leave us alone."

"Skyforce may come back to take out the plane," Melodan said. "I'm taking it up."

Rand blinked. "You?"

"I'm a pilot."

"But not of one of those!"

"We'll see. I'll stay in contact. Let me know if your scouts spot any aircraft."

She thought she'd have to patch the bullet holes in the wing's fabric from the previous day's attack, but the Free Forcers guarding the landing strip had found the repair kit in the cockpit and taken care of that task for her. Now, they helped her turn the plane around, then stood back as she climbed into the pilot's seat. She studied the instruments and recognized them all. *So why don't I feel more confident?* she wondered.

In fact, she felt exactly as she had when making her first solo flight at the Academy: scared to death.

Taking a deep breath, she fired the engine. Once the

propeller spun to life, she released the brakes and opened the throttle.

She began to roll, faster and faster, and realized abruptly just how short the landing strip really was. *What's the rotation speed?* she wondered—then, as the end of the strip raced closer, decided it had better be however fast she was going, and pulled back on the stick.

With no more than five metres to spare, the plane lifted smoothly into the air.

Melodan dared not practice long. Although the Free Forcers had cached a lot of supplies, aviation fuel was not among them. But she had to know which spaceplane manoeuvres could be translated to the biplane. Reflexes were all-important in aerial combat but reflexes honed in a spaceplane might kill her in this primitive biplane.

After twenty minutes, she felt far more confident. Certain violent manoeuvres were out of the question, but the basics were available. The little plane handled beautifully and was much sturdier than it appeared.

She was flying back toward the caves when her earphones crackled. "Two Skyforce planes approaching from the west," Rand's voice said in her ears. "Good luck."

Only two? she thought as her heart started racing. *I'm already in luck.* She spiralled upward. *They'll expect to find the plane on the ground. Their skirmishers will have reported shooting the pilot. They don't know about* me.

Below her, the Skyforcers swung around the peak. *Surprise!* she thought

She dropped into a screaming dive.

MELODAN'S GUNS raked the trailing plane from tail to nose, and it faltered, then disintegrated, scattering wreckage the length of the valley. An instant later, she was on the leader, but he reacted quickly, nosing down, then whipping skyward in the classic half-loop-and-roll known as an Immelman. Melodan followed suit—and her Immelman was tighter. Her opponent was still inverted when her guns found his engine, and flame engulfed him.

Melodan shredded black smoke with a quick victory roll, started to ease down to a landing—then abruptly accelerated. She wasn't done yet, not while the skies were clear of Skyforce and Groundforce was still approaching.

"Where are you going?" Rand demanded in her earphones.

"To greet our visitors!" Melodan replied. She roared over the peak.

Still some kilometres from the top of the pass, she found the Groundforcers, at least three hundred of them, struggling upwards in ragged columns. Some waved as she dived toward them, mistaking her plane for one of those that had flown over them to the attack only minutes before. She smiled grimly and opened fire.

For a long moment, every face below turned toward her in open-mouthed horror, then the columns disintegrated as men and women scrambled for cover or were cut down. Melodan whipped the plane around for a second pass, though this time there were few targets. More holes appeared in her wings, and she fled before the missiles could come out, dropping to a smooth landing on the improvised strip.

She leaped out of the plane almost before it stopped rolling, grinning savagely and feeling more like a gung-ho space pilot than she had in weeks.

But the congratulations that followed from the rest of the Free Forcers began to sound hollow in her ears as the scouts reported on Groundforce's continuing advancement, and she realized how little she had accomplished. And as she sat beside Tor's pallet with Kyla that evening, she wondered how many of the Groundforcers she'd fired on likewise sat beside their wounded friends or grieved their dead ones. *They're no different from Tor*, she thought. *They're just teks drafted from some farm or fishing commune. They're just following orders. They don't deserve to die any more than he does.*

It was an uncomfortable thought, one that had never come to her at the Academy. She wondered if her father had ever felt the same way about the men he killed. Thinking back now on some of the things he'd said—or hadn't said— about his combat experience, she was suddenly sure he had.

Night fell with Groundforce camped just beyond the

peak. Melodan knew that when Skyforce returned, there would be more than two pilots, and they would no longer expect to find the plane helpless.

Before going to bed, she stood in front of the caves, staring up at the stars pricking the sky, and wondered if her message had even reached the rebels. What was happening out there? Where was the Preceptor? Where was the Rebel fleet?

Where was her father?

Was her only accomplishment ensuring that all the Free Forcers died like Vik and Tor?

He's not dead yet! she told herself angrily. *And neither are you! Now get up there and do your job. What kind of fighter pilot are you, anyway?*

Then she had to grin a little because the traditional answer to that question at the Academy was, "The best damn pilot in the galaxy, *sir!*"

You bet, she thought, and as though suddenly bathed in cool water, felt her doubts wash away. Maybe she could have done some things differently. Well, that was always true. But she had done the best she could and now faced the focus of her narrowing options. She would fly and fight—live, or die. The time for choices was past.

She went to bed and slept immediately and well.

RAND NEEDED SLEEP—LONGED for it, in fact—but it would not come. After a time, he gave up and made the trek to the mouth of the cave. He greeted the sentries, then stood by himself, looking up at the stars.

How had all the dreams and plans of the last fifteen years come to this, to a last stand, hopeless except for the faint possibility of a rescue from the stars? It was ludicrous, infuriating, even embarrassing. Events had been taken from his hands. He had lost whatever measure of control he had once had over his fate and that of his followers. He'd gone from being an instigator to a victim, and he hated the feeling of helplessness that now engulfed him.

He'd gone over every event of the past month in his mind. It might have been some comfort had he been able to tell himself that he'd had no other choice than to act as he had, but he knew it wasn't true.

The truth was, Melodan offered him another choice when he first found her—and he rejected it. If he had helped her then, gotten her into the spaceport so she could have sent her message all those weeks ago, the rebels, if they were coming, would already have arrived, before the attack on the valley, before this desperate last stand in the caves. Free Forcers might be dying, but it would be in the fight they had sworn themselves to from the moment they left the service of the Strator, with victory at last in their grasp.

If they died here, in this place, it would be in a final struggle for survival, with no surety that their star-borne allies would ever arrive or that victory could ever be achieved.

Is that how Vik died? Rand thought, looking up at the stars, his hands clenched into fists at his side. *Did he die without hope, without knowing whether his final agony served any purpose?*

"Ask the real question," he whispered. "Did he die hating me?"

He would never know, just as he would never know the dying thoughts of all the Free Forcers who might fall on the morrow.

And what about himself? If he fell, would he truly believe his death had a purpose, that all his struggles, all the pain and suffering, had been worthwhile?

Intellectually, he believed it and could make the arguments to support that belief. But a sea of pain still thundered against the shores of his heart, and in its icy spray, belief froze and withered.

No end could justify the death of his wife and the death of his son, and he knew that f he died on the morrow, that would be the last thought he took with him to the grave.

Head bowed, he returned to his sleepless bed.

THE AIR WAS CLEAR, still, and cold the next morning as Melodan descended to the runway in the pre-dawn twilight. "Go on up to the caves," she told the two Free Forcers stationed there as sentries. "I'll take my chances coming back."

Neither said anything. They both knew just what those chances were.

"Help me turn her around," she said into the silence.

When the plane was in position, each Free Forcer shook her hand before leaving. Melodan climbed into the cockpit and, as the grey light waxed, fired the engine and roared into the air.

She burst out of mountain shade into the first rays of the rising sun. The air was icy but invigorating, and Avalon spread out around her in a wild panorama of rock and sky and trees. For a few minutes, as Melodan circled high above the Free Forcer caves, everything was incredibly peaceful.

But a flash and a billowing cloud of smoke and dust shattered that peace. The attack had begun.

She spiralled down. Groundforcers were spreading into a semi-circle around the Free Forcers' caves, and she shouted their positions to Rand over the radio, then banked, dived, and opened fire.

Men toppled like scythed wheat, but no one ran. Something rode fire and grey smoke past her tail, and more holes suddenly appeared in her already tattered wings. She pulled up, hurtled over the basalt peak—and roared right through the centre of a formation of five Skyforce planes.

Tracers blazed around her as she sideslipped madly, then whipped around and fled back over the peak and low across the valley, the Skyforcers close behind. Something struck the fuselage hard, and the stick began to shudder. *This is it,* Melodan thought, fighting the controls—and then saw, far out over the plains, something huge and dark, misty with distance, descending on Skandar City.

"Rand!" she screamed, but only static answered. The plane dropped violently, and she wondered if she could stay in the air all the way to Skandar. A second lurch toward the trees below brought her heart to her mouth, but the plane responded to her frantic pressure on the stick at last and climbed sluggishly. Tracers streaked overhead, but only for a moment, and she looked back to see the Skyforcers breaking formation and returning to the valley.

They think I'm out of the picture, she thought. *I hope they're wrong.*

And then she looked again at the distant, hovering shape, so familiar and secure—the shape of a Rebel mothership.

The plane continued to descend, every time it dropped, going a little lower than she could climb back. But the land, too, was falling, down to the plains. The question was, which was falling faster?

Ten minutes later, she swept out over farmland, so low she could almost count the stalks of stubble. Skandar was still at least forty kilometres distant. As its towers and the starship's vast bulk grew clearer, she began to think she would succeed, but with ten kilometres still to go, the engine coughed and died, and suddenly her single concern was the row of trees hurtling toward her.

She slammed on flaps and pulled the stick back to the very edge of a stall, fighting for every centimetre of altitude and praying for clear ground beyond the trees.

A moment later, she burst over them, clearing the tallest by only a metre, and an instant after that, touched down in a fallow field, a yellow barn dead ahead.

Melodan braked hard and kicked the rudder left. She heard a sickening snap from the undercarriage, the right wing dropped toward the ground—and then the world whirled around her as the plane flipped onto its back and everything came apart.

ARTEGA SAT at his desk as the sun rose, a glass of his province's finest wine at his side. He didn't normally drink that early in the day, nor did he often waste vidscreen space on images of the dawn, but this was a very special occasion: the final solution to the problem of the Free Forcers was at hand.

The vidscreens on his desk came alive. General Excet, the Groundforce commander, looked out at him. "Strator," Excet said. "Everything is in position for the final assault."

Artega had insisted on giving the command himself. He raised his glass in a toast, sipped from it, and then said, "Very good, General. Commence the attack."

"Yes, Strator!"

The colonel's image vanished, replaced by the feed from the cameras carried by the Groundforcers. As the first missile slammed into the rock above the cave entrance and a Free Forcer staggered and collapsed, Artega raised his glass again. "Farewell, Colonel Rand," he said and settled back to enjoy the show.

Here came the Free Forcers' stolen airplane, as anticipated. He glanced at the positional information on the Skyforce flight providing air support for the attack and smiled. *This should be good*, he thought...

Abruptly, Skandar's voice boomed at a volume reserved for major disasters. "Incoming starship! Incoming starship! Atmospheric penetration! No identification offered! Request human intervention!"

After a moment of stunned immobility, Artega lunged for his desk, his fingers dancing over the controls. On one vidscreen, the embattled valley vanished, to be replaced by a view of the spaceport.

The Strator gaped. Like a mountain impossibly uprooted, a thundercloud of metal hung over the port, dwarfing the towering gantries, its vast shadow enveloping half the field. It was not at all like the pictures Markus had shown him of Preceptorate ships, and it most definitely was not the Preceptor's armoured yacht.

rebels!

Artega shot a glance at the other vidscreens. The Free Forcer plane had been driven from the skies. Groundforce was slowly, surely closing the noose on the caves and their defenders. He still held the reins of control—and that meant the rebels would have to deal with him. They would believe he had been forced to cooperate with the Preceptorate—if no one survived to tell them different. And like the Preceptorate, they would need Skandar's codes, which only he could provide. "Skandar, please transmit to the starship." He paused, then said, "Welcome to Avalon. I am Ekland Artega, Strator of Skandar. Please identify yourself."

A gravelly voice came back. "This is Captain Tuan

Nguyen of the Revolutionary Space Force Mothership *Excalibur*. We have come in response to a message from Pilot First Class Melodan Castille, sent from this planet a little over a week ago, local. I insist on speaking to her."

"Of course, Captain. One moment."

Artega cut the connection and activated his link with Groundforce. A new voice responded, "General Excet's aide."

"This is the Strator," Artega snapped. "Tell the General the terrorists must be neutralized within the hour—at any cost!"

"Yes, Strator!"

Artega returned to the *Excalibur* link. "Captain, I'm afraid we are uncertain of your pilot's whereabouts at this time."

"Strator Artega. We know you have been cooperating with the Preceptorate—we destroyed a Preceptorate cruiser in far orbit upon our arrival. I strongly urge you to begin cooperating with us."

So, Markus was dead. Not necessarily bad news. "I assure you, Captain," Artega replied with just the right injured tone, "I have no love of the Preceptorate. They threatened us. You hardly need threats of your own to gain my help."

"Then where is Pilot Castille?"

"I simply do not have that information," said Artega. "Perhaps we could arrange a meeting and discuss ways to—"

"Strator Artega. I'll give you an hour before my marines follow this link to its source. Nguyen out."

Artega smiled. Time was what he needed—time for Groundforce to complete its eradication of the Free Forcers and Melodan Castille along with them. With her and everyone she had come in contact with dead, there would be no one to contradict Artega's story of cooperating with the Preceptorate under duress. He could still salvage his authority and force the rebels to work with him.

Yes, time was what he needed—and that fool of a captain had just handed him an hour.

MELODAN FOUND herself hanging upside down, still strapped in her seat, cold dirt only a foot or two below her head. For a moment, she hung motionless, wondering dazedly what the sharp smell was stinging her nostrils.

Then she suddenly recognized the smell of alcohol, frantically released her belt, and crashed to the ground. Grunting, she wriggled between fuselage and field, scrambled up, and sprinted away.

With a dull thump, almost-invisible flames enveloped the wreckage, and Melodan threw herself to the ground as the last of the ammunition went up in a burst of orange fire and black smoke and a spray of tracers. Breathing hard, she lay prostrate and stared at the wreckage for a moment. Something tickled her face, and when she wiped at it absent-mindedly, her hand came away red.

Footsteps crunched stubble behind her, and she scrambled up to face a frightened-looking little man with skin tanned to brown leather. "Do you have a horse?" she demanded.

He blinked, and she repeated the question impatiently.

"Well," he said hesitantly, "there's the lord's beast in the barn. But—"

Melodan dashed away. "The Strator will reimburse you!" she shouted over her shoulder and a minute later pounded away bareback on a fine white mare, leaving the old tek staring after her, scratching his head.

Blood from the cut in her forehead stung in her right eye, and she wiped it with the back of her hand, then leaned low over the horse's neck, its wiry mane lashing her cheek.

The towers of Skandar City neared with agonizing slowness, but at last, she clattered up to the spaceport entrance and dismounted, feeling the pulsing of the starship's A-G engines in her bones as she ran to the gate. She had never seen a ship that low in the atmosphere before—the reactors must be near overloading to hold it in place—yet all that power sat there uselessly while her friends died in the mountains. Emblazoned in red letters on the ship's gleaming flank was the name *Excalibur*.

Two Revolutionary marines guarded the gate, and their blazers swung toward her as she approached. "No one allowed in," one growled. "Move!"

"I'm Pilot First Class Melodan Castille," she snapped back. "And if you don't know that name—"

But obviously, they did; one marine dashed into the guard booth while the other lowered his weapon and gaped. "She's here!" she heard. "At the gate! Melodan Castille!" A pause, then, "Yes, sir!" He emerged. "A transport will be here in a second." He held out the microphone in his hand. "Captain Nguyen would like to talk to you."

Melodan took the mike. "Captain Nguyen? Pilot First Class Melodan Castille reporting." She touched the cut on her forehead absently. It had stopped bleeding, but the flesh around it was bruised and sore, and now she was feeling other aches she hadn't noticed before.

The captain sounded harried. "Pilot Castille, report to the spaceplane hangar deck at once. The Preceptor is right behind us. We need every pilot."

Melodan felt a moment's exultation—*this is what I've been waiting for!*—blotted out an instant later by the image of Tor lying wounded in the besieged Free Forcer caves. "With all due respect, sir, I'm needed elsewhere," she said quickly. "There are rebels already engaged in the mountains east of here."

A pause. "Very well. Take whatever you need, but make it quick, Pilot. A lot of the fleet is still tied up at Earth. We may be just a little outnumbered."

"Understood, sir. They only have low tech up there. I think one spaceplane will do the trick—one spaceplane and an Emergency Medical Unit."

"I'll scramble one for you. Good luck, Pilot."

"Thank you, sir."

The line went dead, just as an aircar whistled down beyond the gate. Melodan reached it as its hatch opened, and before it had closed again, the pilot took off, soaring toward the ship.

They swung in through an enormous hatch onto the flight deck, and Melodan burst out of the aircar the moment it stopped. The situation board overlooking the huge gunmetal-grey hangar showed Red Alert 1; spaceplane engines were throbbing, the sharp tang of ozone filled the air, and pilots were awaiting launch. An officer in the white uniform of a deck crew commander met her. "X28 is juiced up for you," he shouted in her ear.

She nodded and ran down the line of needle-sharp prows, dashed up the boarding ladder, and flung herself into the deep black contour chair of the spaceplane's narrow cockpit. She powered up, and the boarding ladder sank out of sight into the metal floor as the cockpit closed and sealed. "X28 to Control. Ready for launch."

"You're clear, X28."

"Thank you, Control." Melodan fired the atmospheric engine and flipped another switch. The wall irised open in front of her, revealing the distant mountains. "Launching!" she cried. She stabbed the catapult button, and acceleration smashed her back into the seat.

At maximum throttle, she hurtled back over the fields and into the mountains, exulting in the power at her command, feeling as if she had just awakened from a long sleep. This was what she had trained for, what she lived for— this was *flying*.

"Watch your scalps, Forcers," she murmured. "I'm coming in *low*."

Already the heads-up display had locked onto the Skyforce planes circling over the caves, marking each with a target symbol. She throttled back, just slightly, and aimed for the middle of the group.

Seconds later, she howled over the valley like a bird of prey with its tail on fire, the stubby-winged spaceplane ripping through the Skyforce biplanes as though they were standing still. The peak loomed, and Melodan shot into a vertical climb, hurtled to ten thousand metres, levelled off inverted, then rolled over into a screaming dive back down toward the battlefield.

She stopped, hovering, while still a thousand metres up, watching the Skyforce planes fleeing the valley to regroup. She let them go. The fighting had stopped, though a pall of smoke hung over everything. Gently she descended to fifty metres. Now she could see that the Groundforce horseshoe had collapsed inward toward the cave. Groundforcers held the rocks around the landing strip, and some were halfway up the slope toward the cave mouth. For a horrible moment, she thought she'd arrived too late, but then she glimpsed movement in the caves.

It was the only movement she glimpsed: every Groundforcer she could see stood transfixed, staring up at her. Melodan glanced at her board and wasn't surprised to see the Skyforce planes reforming high above her. In fact, she'd been counting on it.

They peeled free and dived, one after the other, and an instant later, the tracers arrived. Melodan held the spaceplane absolutely still, listening to the ceramic bullets spend themselves on her armour with a sound like hail. Then she armed her main weapons.

"This should get my point across," she muttered. She pushed the gun control forward and pressed the firing button.

A sun-bright beam ripped into the ground between the front ranks of Groundforce and the cave mouth, and as Melodan eased back on the control, swept a blazing line across the stones. When she released the button, the beam vanished, but the red glow of the slagged rock remained, fading slowly.

In her radar screen, Melodan saw Skyforce departing, while through the cockpit, she saw many of the Ground-forcers doing the same.

She set down on the landing strip, crushing abandoned Groundforce rifles, and tuned her radio to the Free Force frequency. "Rand, do you read me?"

RAND HAD WATCHED Melodan's biplane chased, smoking, from the battlefield and exchanged a glance with Artan at his side. "So much for air support," he said.

"Pilots always take too much credit for infantry victories, anyway," Artan said staunchly, but his face looked pale in the dawn light.

The missile salvo that had opened the Groundforce attack had paused during the brief air battle, but now that they had no fear of being strafed, the Groundforcers became bolder. More missiles screamed up the slope at the huddled Free Forcers, pinning them behind boulders while the Groundforcers slowly advanced. Return fire was spotty, and twice Rand saw Free Forcers rise up to fire, only to fall, screaming, as missile shrapnel took them down.

"Skyforce is coming back!" Artan shouted, and Rand, peering up, saw the planes circling.

"Into the caves!" he ordered. "They'll chew us apart if we stay out here. We'll have to fight them from the cave mouths."

"Yes, sir!" Artan passed the order on through his radio, and the Free Forcers pulled back.

Not all of them made it.

Inside the cave, Rand saw Kyla, rifle in hand, coming up the tunnel. "You should be with your brother!" he shouted to her above the din of explosions and gunfire.

"I'm not doing him or you any good down there," she shouted back. "I joined the Free Forcers to fight, Colonel!"

It was far too late to worry about protecting people, Rand thought. "Then get up there!" he ordered, and with a grim salute, she hurried on.

Rand made his way back to the infirmary, already crowded, with more wounded being brought in. They had only one trained medic, plus the two assistants the medic he'd trained himself, and their meagre medical supplies were rapidly running out.

I doubt it matters, Rand thought. *If we can't hold off Groundforce, none of us will leave these caves alive.*

Oddly, the thought brought him a measure of peace. All choices were truly out of his hands, now.

Death is the end of responsibility.

He went back into the tunnel, unslung his rifle, made sure its magazine was full, then returned to the battle.

<hr>

KYLA LAY behind a rock just outside the main entrance of the cave, firing at the dimly glimpsed Groundforcers on the far side of the smoke-filled ravine. Bullets whined over her head, occasionally shattering on stones within an arms-length of her, but she hadn't been hit yet.

A missile slammed into the slope above her, and fist-sized rocks cascaded down on her, but she hardly felt them. She fired, reloaded, and kept firing, and two thoughts kept recycling endlessly in her head, alternating with each pull of the trigger...

For Vik, she thought. Bang! *For Tor*. Bang! *For Vik*. Bang! *For Tor*. Bang! *For Vik*...

And then, suddenly, Groundforce wasn't on the other side of the ravine, it was on *this* side, crouched on the other side of the fang-like rocks that had once been the Free Force battlements. Rifle muzzles flashed in the smoke. Something stung her cheek like a hot bee, and she felt blood trickling down to her chin, then dripping from it.

This was better, with Groundforce on this side. Now she could really aim. She fired, saw a Groundforcer fall backward, rifle flying from her hands; fired again, and sent another Groundforcer running for better cover, only to be cut down by someone else's bullet before he made it. She aimed again...

...and something roared over the ravine like a tornado, smoke swirling in its wake. A powerful shockwave shook the ground, making the pebbles dance around her.

The sound changed pitched, dwindled skyward, then came roaring back, and suddenly she saw its source, a silvery craft, needle-nosed, stub-winged, grim-looking nozzles and barrels protruding from it, antennae bristling around its glassed-in cockpit.

The shooting stopped. Groundforcers and Free Forcers alike stared at the apparition.

Skyforce came buzzing in, firing. The new craft just hung there, ignoring the tracers slashing around it.

Then a nozzle on its underbelly swivelled, and a blinding blue-white beam whipped across the ravine, drawing a glowing line of molten rock.

Groundforce broke and fled. Some of the Free Forcers might have done the same if they'd had anywhere to run. But Kyla rose to her feet, fierce joy burning in her heart as brightly as the beam that had saved them. "Melodan!" she cried.

RAND WATCHED the routing of Groundforce with something approaching disbelief. He'd been resigned to the inevitable destruction of himself and his friends and followers. Now, it appeared, he'd have to start thinking about the future again. *I guess I'm not quite through with responsibility yet.*

"Rand, do you read me?" a voice crackled from Artan's radio. Artan handed it to him.

"Rand here," he said. "Melodan, I presume?"

He could almost hear her grin. "The Revolutionary Space Force has arrived, as promised!"

"So I see. And my heartfelt thanks to them. Melodan, there are a lot of wounded down here. Can you—"

"Help is already on its way. I'm coming down, Colonel. Melodan out."

Rand watched the spaceplane set down in the ravine, untroubled by the now heavily cratered airstrip. Free Forcers plunged down the slope to greet Melodan, but Rand stayed put.

They'd won. They *wouldn't* all die, not today.

If only he'd acted sooner, Vik might not have died, either.

He watched the others celebrate. He didn't join in.

———

KYLA WAS among the first to reach the spaceplane. As the cockpit opened and Melodan climbed down to the ground, Kyla flung her rifle away and threw her arms around her friend.

The other Free Forcers milled around, touching the vehicle and Melodan as though they couldn't believe either of them were really there. A flight of spaceplanes screamed high overhead, contrails shining white, and Melodan looked up. "What's happening?" Kyla cried above the general din.

"The Preceptor," Melodan replied.

"Shouldn't you be out there?"

"No," Melodan said firmly. "This plane has to be right where it is." She pointed to the east, and Kyla, squinting, saw a boxy shape, glittering in the morning sun, soaring toward them through the air. "That's an Emergency Medical Unit— sort of a movable hospital. It's tracking my signal here."

Emergency Medical... "Tor!" she whispered.

Melodan seized her shoulders. "He's still alive, isn't he?"

"I don't know! I haven't checked on him since..." She broke free and scrambled up the slope, reaching the caves as the EMU landed beside the spaceplane in a swirl of dust.

The medic looked up, face haggard, as she burst into the infirmary, thick with the stench of blood, urine, and vomit. "What's happening? I heard a roar, then—"

"Help has arrived," Kyla said. "Medical help."

"What? But how—"

Kyla pushed past him and knelt beside Tor. For a heart-stopping moment, she thought he had quit breathing, but then his chest moved. Only a little...but that was enough. He still lived!

The crowded infirmary suddenly got a lot more crowded as Melodan burst in, followed by four men and two women lugging white cases marked with the age-old red cross. The medic's face lit up with disbelieving joy, and he ran to meet the new arrivals.

"He's still alive!" Kyla said as Melodan joined her. One of the EMU medics gently pushed her aside and pulled back Tor's blanket, attaching sensors to his chest, arms, and forehead.

The medic scanned flickering readouts on a datapad and frowned. "We've got to get him to the ship as soon as possi-ble," she said. "The medic here says he's the one in the most immediate danger, but there are still injured people outside. And the EMU will only hold four."

"I'll take him," Melodan said at once. "In the spaceplane. Then I'll come back with a transport."

The medic nodded. "Right." She moved on to the next pallet.

Melodan grabbed a stretcher leaning against the cave wall. "Can the two of us carry him?" she asked Kyla.

"He's my brother," Kyla said. She helped Melodan ease Tor onto the stretcher. As they picked him up, she looked down at his thin, pale face. Yes, whatever else he had been or had done, he was her brother.

She hoped she'd still get a chance to tell him that.

Melodan helped Kyla carry Tor back out through the haze-filled tunnel, and with the willing assistance of some of the Free Forcers standing by, eased him into the back seat of the spaceplane, where a weapons officer rode when the plane was on a space-to-ground mission. Melodan climbed into the pilot's seat. "I'll take care of him," she promised Kyla.

More spaceplanes broke the sound barrier somewhere over the plain, and Kyla glanced up. "Won't you be heading out there?"

In her memory, Melodan heard her own voice speaking to a friend back at the Academy. *I want to go where the action is. I want to prove to my father I can fly...*

"I've got an assignment on Avalon," she said out loud. "It's not finished yet." She sealed the cockpit and lifted, and as she rocketed toward Skandar City, called, "*Excalibur*, X28."

"Go ahead, X28."

"I need a medium-sized transport. We've got a lot of wounded up here."

A pause. "All we have available is a four-place shuttle, X28."

"That will have to do."

"Acknowledged." Another pause. "X28, stand by for Captain Nguyen."

"Pilot Castille?" the captain said a moment later. "We could use you in space."

"I'm sorry, sir, but a lot of people in the mountains could die if we don't get them to the ship."

"Who are these people, Pilot?"

That needed an hour's answer—or only one word. "Friends, sir."

Silence. Then, "Very well. There's no one else to spare, so I guess you've just volunteered for ambulance duty. I hope we'll be able to stay on station here."

"How are things going out there, sir?"

"Could be better. Captain Nguyen out."

And so, while the last battle of the Revolution blazed through the space surrounding Avalon, Melodan ferried the wounded from the mountains to *Excalibur*. Tor was whisked away to surgery the moment she landed the spaceplane, and the doctor who took charge of him had no time for questions or answers. Melodan turned over the spaceplane and returned to the mountains in the luxurious *Dagger*, the captain's gig. Its plush seats and carpet were bloodstained and dusty by the end of the fourth trip, when Melodan delivered the last of the injured Free Forcers to the starship, and still, she wasn't finished, for then came a flood of Groundforcers, carried across the ravine by their hesitant comrades, willing to face the now-silent crowd of Free Forcers to save their friends.

On every flight, Melodan longed to call Captain Nguyen and find out what was happening in space but knew she could not disturb him to satisfy her own curiosity. Instead, she watched the sky for Swordcraft.

On her last trip, she transported Kyla. Her cheek wound had been stitched and bandaged by the medics, so she was not in need of further treatment, but Melodan knew she would want to be as close to Tor as possible.

The Avalon girl watched the swelling bulk of the mothership in awe. "It's unbelievable," she whispered.

"But real," Melodan assured her. "And right now, they're saving Tor's life on board." *I hope*, she added silently.

She landed the gig with relief. The EMU came in a moment later, and as its wounded and the two she had carried were spirited away, Melodan took a deep breath and set off resolutely across the grey deck toward the X28, waiting where she had parked it, now fully refuelled and re-armed.

Kyla ran after her. "Melodan, wait—"

"They're still fighting out there," Melodan said.

"But you're exhausted!"

It was true. Melodan felt fatigue gripping every muscle, every brain cell, but it didn't matter. They had accomplished nothing if the Preceptorate claimed Avalon. "It's my duty," she said. "Go to your brother."

Kyla grabbed her arm and pulled her around. Melodan braced herself for further protests, but instead, Kyla only stared into her eyes for a moment, said, "Good luck," and hugged her. Melodan hugged her back, then turned and trudged to the spaceplane and hauled herself wearily into the cockpit.

"X28 available for combat," she said into her microphone as she powered up. "Awaiting orders."

"X28, proceed at once to—" Abruptly, silence fell.

"I didn't copy, Control."

It was the captain's voice that came back. "Pilot Castille, I'm afraid we've got another emergency for you."

"Sir?"

"A man called Ekland Artega—the Strator of Skandar City—do you know him?"

What could the Strator attempt with a starship hanging over his head? "I know *of* him, sir."

"He just contacted us. He's holding one of your Free Forcers hostage."

Melodan blinked. A Free Forcer? Hildar, maybe? But what did he hope to accomplish by that? "Who, sir?

"A boy named Vik."

After Captain Nguyan signed off, Artega spent the next half-hour watching the battle in the highlands as Groundforce pressed the attack. But as the time neared for him to contact Captain Nguyen again, he saw, on one of his peripheral screens, something that drew his attention: a young woman riding up to the spaceport gate on horseback.

"Skandar."

"Yes, Strator?"

"Identify the woman at the spaceport gate."

There was a pause. "Name unknown. Subject's only previous entry in memory is in vidrecord GF-176Y."

"Display, Screen 5."

The indicated screen lit, and Artega felt all his plans crumbling into ashes.

The woman who was even then being ferried to the *Excalibur* had last been recorded by a Skybase surveillance camera as she climbed into the Free Forcers' stolen Skyforce plane.

"Melodan Castille," Artega snarled. There was no need

now to contact Captain Nguyen again. The captain's marines would be coming for sure. Nor was there any need to continue the bloodshed in the high valley, but Artega made no move to stop it. He had no desire to.

His hope of retaining power was lost; that was clear. His priorities shifted like lightning. Now his personal safety was paramount. To assure it, he needed something to bargain with.

The Skandar codes, he thought. *The Skandar codes, and—*

From a compartment in his desk, he removed a holstered handgun. Belting it on, he left his office at a brisk walk, ignoring worried glances from his staff. At the single entrance to the warren of his headquarters stood two Peaceforcer guards. "I want more Peaceforcers up here at once," he ordered. "This office is about to be attacked!"

"Yes, sir!" one snapped smartly and turned to an intercom. Artega inserted his keycard into the lock and swept out, leaving the other Peaceforcer staring after him.

The moment he was out of sight, he abandoned decorum and dashed to the nearest elevator, descending to the hospital level. He ran past three startled nurses and burst into the room where Vik sat in a wheelchair by his bed, grinning out the window at the *Excalibur*. As Artega entered, something winged and shining shot from the starship's vast flank and screamed toward the mountains.

Artega seized the handles of the wheelchair and jerked it sharply back. "Artega!" Vik gasped, half-twisting to look at him. Then he smiled. "Problems?"

The Strator ignored him. Pushing the wheelchair, he banged out into the corridor again and down toward the office of Dr. Methon, who emerged as they approached. "What are you doing?" the doctor exploded. "He's too weak for—"

"He's recovered enough for my purposes," Artega snarled. "I'm taking over your office. I recommend you leave the building."

The doctor hesitated, then grimaced and left.

Once inside, the Strator locked the door firmly, shoved Vik's chair against the wall, and sat behind the doctor's desk, a smaller version of his own. Then he waited.

"Scared?" Vik asked.

"One more word, and I'll gag you," Artega snapped.

An hour passed. Two. Three. Periodically something roared overhead—more of the flying things from the starship, Artega supposed. But that wasn't what he was listening for.

It came at last: muffled thunder elsewhere in the building that shook the whole structure. It went on for ten minutes, then suddenly stopped.

"Skandar, open link from here through my office to the *Excalibur*." Skandar did not acknowledge, but a green light appeared on the doctor's communication panel, near the centre of the desk. "Captain Nguyen, this is Strator Artega."

"Surrender, Artega," the captain said. "We've taken your office. Five of your men died. Quit now before anyone else does."

"If you've taken my office, Captain, you know I'm not in it. And if you don't want anyone else to die, then you will bargain with me. I'm holding a hostage, Captain. A Free Forcer boy named Vik. Your precious pilot knows him very well—he helped her get into the spaceport and summon you." Artega smiled. "And I have something else you need,

Captain. I have the programming codes for Skandar. You can't run the spaceport or the city without them."

A pause. "What do you want, Artega?"

"Safety, Captain. I want assurances I will not be punished. In return, I will spare the boy."

"What about the codes?"

"The codes I keep. I like being essential—it makes me feel safe."

Another pause. "I'll have to think about this, Artega."

"Don't think too long, Captain. Even if I kill the boy, I still have the codes. Artega out." He turned and smiled at the hatred in Vik's eyes. "Skandar, please keep me informed as to the whereabouts of any armed forces in the building."

Silence. Artega frowned. "Skandar?"

"Lose someone?" asked Vik.

"Quiet!" Of course, there was no reason for Skandar to have a voicebox in this office. But there should be a vidscreen. Artega searched the surface of the desk and found a screen—but it was blank. "Skandar, activate vidscreen at this location."

Nothing.

Artega drew his handgun and pointed it at the boy. "At least I've still got you."

Vik eyed him coldly.

They waited in silence for another fifteen or twenty minutes. Finally, Artega could wait no longer. "Skandar, contact *Excalibur*." The link opened, and the Strator smiled, reassured. Skandar was still there, and still in his control. "Captain Nguyen, I need a decision."

He heard a noise outside the door. He'd just started to turn toward it when it exploded inward in smoke and flame.

Kyla, feeling lost and alone, had just turned to leave the landing bay when the spaceplane's cockpit suddenly popped open. "Kyla! Artega has Vik! He's *alive!*"

Her heart skipped a beat; then, she was running across the metal floor to join Melodan in the X28.

They roared out of the landing bay and banked toward the heart of the city. Melodan destroyed a small park with her landing rockets, then both of them clambered out of the spaceplane and dashed toward the city's Central Tower, the tall white doors that sealed its entrance crumpled and blackened by someone who had gone before them.

Inside, the marble lobby swarmed with RSF marines, who directed them to the twenty-eighth floor. They got off the elevators to find themselves in a white-tiled hospital corridor where more marines, incongruous in black battle-armour, crouching outside a door.

The nearest marine looked up as they emerged from the elevator and hurriedly jumped up, grabbed their arms, and pulled them down—just as something exploded and the door blasted inward.

The marines burst into the room. The one that had grabbed them tried to hold Kyla back, but she pulled free and ran to the door. "Vik!" she called...and stopped.

Vik sat in a wheelchair, very much alive, and her heart leaped again to see him—but standing beside him, gun aimed at his head, was a man she'd never seen before but recognized instantly from countless photographs: Ekland Artega, Strator of Skandar.

THE BLAST TOPPLED ARTEGA BACKWARD. He rolled and came up with his gun aimed at Vik as two men in black armour burst into the office, the aiming lasers on their weapons drawing small red lights on his chest. "Move, and I kill him!" Artega cried.

Everyone froze for an instant. The red aiming beams never wavered, but the armoured men came no closer. In the corridor beyond, Artega saw Melodan, another girl he didn't know, and more marines. "Captain, call them off!" Artega shouted. "Or—"

He got no further. His attention had been on the door. Only when something struck him from the side did he realize he should have watched Vik as well. He fired as he fell, his gun shockingly loud in the enclosed space, then, in a fury, flung the wounded boy away and staggered to his feet.

The gun was still in his hand, but no longer aimed at his hostage, who lay where Artega had thrown him. The Strator hoped he'd killed him.

One of the aiming lasers moved from his heart to his head, glowing between his eyes. "Move, and you're dead," the gun's owner growled. Melodan and the other girl rushed into the room and knelt beside Vik.

Artega ignored them. "Captain Nguyen," he said to the still-open link. "Kill me, and you lose Skandar."

And then came the final blow.

"We've already deactivated your artificial intelligence, Artega," Nguyen said. "You really should have updated its security systems sometime in the last century."

Artega's heart stumbled, stabbing his chest with sudden, sharp pain. "Skandar is dead?"

"If you want to call it that. We'll be installing our own. In the meantime, the ship's computer has full control of all of Skandar's databases and sensors."

"But...the communications link..."

"Activated by our computer. How do you think we found you?"

The gun dropped from Artega's limp hand, and he sagged against the doctor's desk, offering no resistance as the marines came for him.

As Kyla knelt over Vik, he groaned and opened his eyes, and relief flooded through her. Without thinking, she bent over and kissed him, and after a moment he returned the kiss enthusiastically.

Melodan cleared her throat, and Kyla, embarrassed, pulled back. Vik blinked up at her. "I should get shot more often," he said.

"Excuse us, miss," said one of the marines. "We have orders to transport the boy to sickbay on the *Excalibur*. There's an EMU waiting outside."

They gently lifted Vik onto a stretcher. All the way out of the building, Kyla walked beside him, holding his hand. It was like a miracle: all the horrible things that had happened, the things that had numbed her and frozen her soul, were being undone. Vik still lived. Tor at least had a fighting chance. The Strator, who had almost killed them all, had been defeated. Skandar, who had coldly controlled their lives from birth, had been deactivated.

Her heart was so full she couldn't speak. She contented herself with holding Vik's hand and not letting go.

As they crossed the street to the EMU, four spaceplanes swooped low overhead, each rolling once, one after the other, the sound of their engines echoing back from the empty towers all around them.

Melodan whooped.

"What is it?" Kyla asked.

"We've won!" Melodan grabbed her and hugged her so tight she saw spots in front of her eyes. "Everything's going to be all right! It's all over!"

Kyla had forgotten about the battle in space. The Preceptorate still didn't seem real to her. The idea that ships from other worlds would soon be visiting Avalon on a regular basis seemed impossible. But she had no trouble summoning a smile for her friend's excitement, and it seemed like another good excuse to kiss Vik, so she did.

Back aboard the *Excalibur*, they accompanied Vik's gurney to sickbay, Melodan plying him with questions about what had happened while they were separated. But as they approached the sickbay door, Kyla looked up and saw the medic who had taken charge of Tor, and her heart jumped. She suddenly felt certain he brought bad news, that she would pay a horrible price for allowing herself to believe...

She squeezed Vik's right hand. Melodan gripped and squeezed her left.

The medic glanced at Kyla and Vik, blinked, then looked at Melodan. "He's going to be all right," he said. "We'll keep him unconscious for a day or two yet, but he'll survive."

Kyla let out a breath she didn't realize she'd been holding. The corridor spun around her, and she would have fallen to her knees if Melodan hadn't caught her. "Easy! Tor's all right, but are you?"

"I'm fine," Kyla whispered. She straightened and took a deep breath, feeling as if a massive weight she hadn't even realized she'd been carrying had been removed from her shoulders. "I really am. For the first time in a long time."

"Good," Vik said, then exclaimed, "Hey!" as the medic wheeled him away.

Kyla took a few steps after him, then reluctantly stopped as the medic looked at her and shook his head. "We'll talk later!" she called after him.

She had all the time in the world, she realized. All the time in the world...

It was a strange feeling, but she thought she could get to like it.

Melodan suddenly laughed. "Rand!" she said. "We've got to tell Rand! Let's get to communications." She turned, then stopped. "Or better yet...come on." With Kyla following cheerfully behind, she set off down the corridor.

RAND HAD OVERSEEN the transporting of all the wounded. Now he had begun the process of packing up the rest of his followers and their supplies for transport back to Skandar City...only a temporary relocation, according to many of the Free Forcers, if he could still call them that. Next spring, they were saying, they planned to return to their valley to rebuild and replant.

Rand couldn't think that far ahead. Once the Free Forcers were officially disbanded, he didn't know what he'd do or where he'd go. Leading the Free Forcers had given shape to his life, along with his wife and son. First his wife had been stripped from him, then his son, and now...

The dream of freedom he'd had when he'd started the Free Forcers had come true, and he was startled to find that freedom frightened him.

Would you rather be dead? part of him asked. *You were well-enough resigned to that.*

He had no answer. Instead, he tried to concentrate on the job at hand and leave tomorrow to take care of itself.

Artan came up beside him as he packed unused missiles back into their crate. "Sir, I just received a communication from Melodan. She's returning to the valley to pick you up and transport you to the *Excalibur*."

"The what? Oh, the starship." Rand stood up, brushing dirt from his hands. "Did she say why? There's still a lot of work to be done here."

"No, sir. Only that it's important."

Rand sighed. "Very well." He sealed the crate, then went to the screened-off corner of the cave he'd made his quarters to gather his few belongings. Among them was a picture of Lissa and Vik, taken not long before Lissa died. He looked at that one a long time before slipping it into his backpack.

Melodan was close-lipped on the trip back to *Excalibur*. "I'm sorry, Colonel, but I'm not allowed to tell you anything," she said, and he was reminded that she served commanders other than him...if he could still call himself a commander, now that his war was over.

He'd never flown before. He found the sensation unpleasant. The size of *Excalibur* astounded him as they approached, and he was glad when at last he climbed down from the spaceplane inside the cavernous landing bay. Strictly speaking, they might still be airborne, but in here, he could at least make believe they were on the ground.

Holding his backpack in one hand, he waited expectantly for Melodan. "Follow me, Colonel," she said, and he did so, through corridors and up lifts, until he was thoroughly lost. Finally, they passed into an area he recognized as a hospital and reached a closed door. Kyla stood outside.

Rand thought he understood. "Is it Tor?" he said grimly. "Kyla, I'm so sorry..."

"No, sir," she said. "Tor is going to be all right. It's another Free Forcer. He insists on seeing you."

"Well, let's not keep him waiting." Rand took a deep breath, trying to summon up the mask of the perfect commander he'd perfected over the years, though it had begun to slip in recent weeks, and opened the door.

The mask and all his composure shattered when he saw his son sitting up in bed, looking at him.

He never remembered crossing the floor. Vik was suddenly in his arms, and he was weeping openly in a way he'd never allowed himself in all his years with the Free Forcers...and Vik didn't try to pull free or push him away. Instead, he wept, too. Father and son clung to each other, and behind him, Rand heard the door close as Kyla and Melodan discretely withdrew.

When at last he could control himself, Rand pulled back, though he kept his hands on his son's shoulders. "We thought you were dead. All of us. I thought I'd gotten you killed, too!"

"I thought I was dead, too, Dad," Vik said. "I knew I'd been shot. The next thing I knew, I was in the Strator's hospital, with Strator Artega himself leaning over me." He looked down. "Father, I...I was the one who told them where the caves were. They drugged me. I tried to fight it, honestly, I did, but...I'm sorry. I'm sorry I was so weak."

"It's all right," Rand said and meant it. "It wasn't your fault. And it's all over now, anyway."

"There's something else I'm sorry for, Father." This time, Vik raised his head and met Rand's gaze squarely. "I'm sorry that I blamed you for Mother's death. I know it wasn't really your fault. I've always known. I just...hurt, so much, and...I guess I had to blame someone, and you were closest. I thought...I'd always thought you could do anything, that nothing bad could happen to us because you were my father and Commander of the Free Forcers. I never...I never wanted to let you be human."

Rand hugged his son again. "I blamed myself just as much," he whispered. "I didn't want to admit I was human, either. I guess we both know better now." He straightened. "The war is over, son. I'm resigning as commander of the Free Forcers. They don't exist anymore anyway. From now on, I'm going to concentrate on just being your father." He tried on a smile. It fit pretty well. "I think that's job enough for any man."

Vik smiled back, and with that smile, the future no longer held any fear for Rand, once commander of the Free Forcers, now just a father.

With a *lot* of catching up to do.

MELODAN AND KYLA, giggling like children over how they'd surprised Colonel Rand, went back to the flight deck to pick up the gear Melodan had left in the X28—and emerged into either a riot or the start of a three-day party. "What happened?" Melodan shouted above the din at one of the dozens of red-uniformed RSF pilots milling about. "I thought we'd already won the battle."

"We did, but the Preceptor got away," the pilot shouted. "One of our flights intercepted his ship at the last possible moment. Its reactor blew. The Preceptor's dead! It's all over!" He threw his helmet into the air. "*It's all over!*"

Melodan whooped and swung Kyla into an impromptu dance, then collapsed with her, laughing and exhausted, against the nearest bulkhead. "I don't know about you, but what I need now is food!" Melodan said. "And a shower. Everything but sleep—I don't think I could."

Kyla grinned at her a little weakly. "I could…"

"Not yet!" Melodan cried. "I've got—"

"Plans," she had intended to say, but she was cut off by an announcement over the ship's intercom. "Pilot First Class Melodan Castille, Pilot First Class Melodan Castille, report to debriefing room Z4 immediately. Repeat, Pilot First Class Melodan Castille, report to debriefing room Z4."

Melodan made a face. "The military catches up with me." She sighed. "Oh, well. Want to come along?"

"I really should get back to sickbay."

Melodan started to tell her that Tor would not wake for hours but stopped. *She's been through enough. All she wants to do is sit by her brother and let the fact sink in that he's going to survive—and she is, too.* "Good idea. Can you find your way?"

"I think so."

"I'll look you up later."

Kyla nodded and hurried back down the corridor.

Debriefing room Z4 was located near the bridge, and as she passed dozens of hurrying officers, all in neatly pressed white, Melodan became more and more aware of her own less-than-regulation dress. She also began to wonder who she was about to meet and cringed a little at the thought that it could be Captain Nguyen, Fleet Admiral Norseth, or even a Councillor, with her looking like something that had crawled from under a rock. Her tattered Free Forcer fatigues were dusty and spattered with blood and mud and aviation fuel, and she hadn't had a bath since that night in Lady Moldar's apartment.

If you can face Skyforce at five-to-one odds, you can face a mere admiral, she admonished herself as she reached the debriefing room's door. Straightening her shoulders, she pressed the access button.

The door slid open. She stepped into the half-lit room beyond.

Her father stood up from behind the long black table. "Hello, Melodan," he said.

Ten years dissolved, and Melodan was suddenly a little girl again. She ran to him and hugged him as tight as she could, pulling back only after a long time and brushing at her eyes with her fingers. "I'm sorry, sir..."

"Sir?" her father said quietly. "A little formal, don't you think?"

Melodan lowered her head. "I don't know if I'm here for a family reunion or a dressing-down." She found she was trembling. It had been so long since she had seen him, and they had grown so far apart—and as she remembered why, old resentment flared. "I haven't seen you for a long time."

"I know. I'm sorry."

"Oh, I understood. You didn't approve of my becoming a pilot." She closed her eyes. "Maybe you were right. I lost my scoutship as soon as I entered the system. I had no escape course set, and when I ran into that Preceptorate ship..."

"You survived. If you survive your first major mistake, you've got a good chance of surviving your minor ones."

"I worried about how you would react. All I've ever wanted was to make you as proud of me as I was of you—the great pilot, the war hero. I wanted to be just like you."

Her father silently motioned for her to sit in one of the plain black chairs around the table, and she did so, not meeting his eyes. He remained standing, going to a cupboard and taking out a bottle of something green and sparkling. "Drink?" he asked.

"No, thank you."

He nodded, poured himself a glass, and re-stopped the bottle. Only then did he sit down opposite her. He took a slow sip of the drink, then set it down on the table's polished surface. "You're right. I didn't approve of your becoming a pilot," he said quietly. "I thought, 'All my life I've been fighting to keep my home and family safe from the Preceptorate, and now my daughter wants to throw that security away.'" He shook his head. "I was being selfish. I realized it when they told me you had never reported back from Avalon. All I could think of was how we'd grown apart. And when we did hear from you—I made sure I was assigned to this ship." He looked up at her. "I *am* proud of you, Melodan. Believe me."

Melodan swallowed an enormous lump in her throat. "Did we really win?"

"We did—thanks to you." He grinned at her suddenly. "My dear daughter, you are going to be more of a hero than I've ever been. *Now,* are you satisfied?"

Melodan stood, went to him, and kissed him on the cheek. "Perfectly," she said.

TOR WOKE SLOWLY, without any idea of where he was. He blinked up at the white ceiling. Tubes ran into his right arm and something was clipped to his nostrils. A black box on his left beeped softly in time to his heartbeat. Vidscreens above his bed flickered, green traces slowly crawling across their faces.

A hospital, then. But...how?

He remembered...the boy...someone shooting...he'd run to save the boy, and then...nothing.

But he remembered everything before that, with painful clarity. The tekfarm...Parl...the attack on the valley...and Kyla...Kyla, avoiding him, hardly able to look at him, never speaking...

He closed his eyes again. It might have been better if he'd never woken up.

"Tor?"

He opened his eyes, and there she stood, looking down at him, her left cheek bandaged.

Kyla, the sister he had betrayed.

He tried to talk, but his throat was too dry; he only managed a croak. She smiled at him—*smiled* at him!—and brushed his hair back from his forehead with fingers that trembled a little. "It's all right, Tor," she said softly. "It's all right. You're in the infirmary of a Rebel starship. The Strator is in custody. Skandar has been deactivated. The Preceptor is dead. There'll be no more lords and ladies...no more Battlefield. The teks are free. And you helped make it happen."

His head swam. It was too much to take in. The words slithered past his understanding like slippery fish. But one thing came through clearly, and he clung to it, held it close, and let it ease him back down into peaceful rest.

It was the one thing he'd thought he'd never see again: the look of love in his sister's eyes.

———

MELODAN PILOTED the X28 west from Skandar, woods, fields, and tekfarms flashing beneath the spaceplane's wings. "Are you sure you won't come with me?" she said. "You don't have to stay on Avalon now, you know. The whole galaxy is open to you."

"It's also not going anywhere," Kyla said from the back cockpit, her voice clear in Melodan's headphones. "I'm a Free Forcer, Melodan. That means a lot to me. We have to show the teks they can live free, without lords and ladies and Strators and AIs telling them what to do: Colonel Rand, and Vik, and the rest of us who fought up there in the mountains —and survived." She was quiet for a moment, then said, "Tor will go with you."

Melodan nodded, though she knew Kyla couldn't see her. In the last two weeks, Tor and Kyla had made their peace with one another, but she doubted Tor could ever be entirely at peace with himself. Not on this world. It held too many ghosts.

"He'll miss you," she said.

"I'll miss him, too."

They were silent for several minutes while Melodan gave her attention to landing on a gravel road. Kyla climbed out the moment the cockpit opened and walked slowly across the road to stare up at a locked gate in a fence of plastic mesh. Down the long path beyond it, Melodan glimpsed farm buildings and hesitant teks coming to investigate.

Kyla took a cutter from her belt and touched the lock. There was a flash, and the portal swung silently open. Then Kyla came back to the spaceplane.

"That's it?" Melodan asked.

Kyla smiled. "It's a beginning."

EDDIE WILLETT is a younger version of EDWARD WILLETT, the award-winning author of more than sixty books of science fiction, fantasy, and nonfiction for readers of all ages, including twelve novels for DAW Books, most recently the humorous outer-space adventure *The Tangled Stars*. *Marseguro* (DAW Books) won the Aurora Award (honouring Canadian science fiction and fantasy) for Best Long-Form Work in English and his young adult fantasy *Spirit Singer* (also available from Shadowpaw Press) won a

Saskatchewan Book Award for best book by a Regina author. Several other of his books have been shortlisted for those and other awards, including *Star Song*, his most recent novel for Shadowpaw Press, which was shortlisted for the Aurora Award for Best Young Adult Novel.

His nonfiction runs the gamut from science books to biographies to history, and he hosts the Aurora Award-winning podcast *The Worldshapers*, in which he talks to other science fiction and fantasy authors about their creative process. A former newspaper reporter and editor, Ed is also a professional actor and singer. He lives in Regina, Saskatchewan, with his wife, Margaret Anne Hodges, P.Eng., a past president of the Association of Professional Engineers and Geoscientists of Saskatchewan. They have one daughter and a much younger black Siberian cat, after whom Shadowpaw Press is named.

You can find Ed online at www.edwardwillett.com.

 facebook.com/edward.willett

 twitter.com/ewillett

 instagram.com/edwardwillettauthor

Thickwood

By Gayle M. Smith

The Emir's Falcon

By Matt Hughes

One Lucky Devil

The First World War Memoirs of Sampson J. Goodfellow

By Sampson J. Goodfellow

Paths to the Stars

Twenty-Two Fantastical Tales of Imagination

By Edward Willett

Shapers of Worlds

Shapers of Worlds Volume II

Shapers of Worlds Volume III

Science fiction and fantasy by authors who were guests on the
award-winning podcast *The Worldshapers*

Star Song

By Edward Willett

SHADOWPAW PRESS *Reprise*

New editions of notable, previously published books

Stay

By Katherine Lawrence

Duatero

By Brad C. Anderson

Blue Fire

By E.C. Blake

Phases

By Belinda Betker

Legend of Sarah

Cat's Pawn

Cat's Gambit

Cat's Game

By Leslie Gadallah

The Crow Who Tampered With Time

Backwater Mystic Blues

By Lloyd Ratzlaff

The Shards of Excalibur Series

The Peregrine Rising Duology

Spirit Singer

From the Street to the Stars

By Edward Willett

Dollybird

By Anne Lazurko

Small Reckonings

By Karin Melberg Schwier

The Ghosts of Spiritwood

By Martine Noël-Maw